FRONTIER FURY

In a berserk rage, Finn threw himself at Fargo, stabbing, thrusting, swinging, raining frenzied strokes that Fargo barely dodged, ducked or blocked.

Fargo was forced back, and was taken unawares when his left foot came down on one of the rifles, throwing him off-balance. Before he could recover, Finn swung again, and although Fargo brought the Arkansas Toothpick up in time to counter the blow, the force sent him toppling.

Fargo hit on his shoulders and rolled as he landed. As he rose he ripped a handful of grass out by the roots. Finn snarled and pounced, stabbing at Fargo's throat. Skipping aside, Fargo flung the grass in Finn's face. The roustabout instinctively recoiled. For a moment Finn's guard was down, and it was all Fargo needed. He sank the Tooth-pick to the hilt in Finn's belly and wrenched it out again. . . .

THE
TRAILSMAN
#284

DAKOTA
PRAIRIE PIRATES

by

Jon Sharpe

Ø

A SIGNET BOOK

SIGNET
Published by New American Library, a division of
Penguin Group (USA) Inc., 375 Hudson Street,
New York, New York 10014, USA
Penguin Group (Canada), 10 Alcorn Avenue, Toronto,
Ontario M4V 3B2, Canada (a division of Pearson Penguin Canada Inc.)
Penguin Books Ltd., 80 Strand, London WC2R 0RL, England
Penguin Ireland, 25 St. Stephen's Green, Dublin 2,
Ireland (a division of Penguin Books Ltd.)
Penguin Group (Australia), 250 Camberwell Road, Camberwell, Victoria 3124,
Australia (a division of Pearson Australia Group Pty. Ltd.)
Penguin Books India Pvt. Ltd., 11 Community Centre, Panchsheel Park,
New Delhi - 110 017, India
Penguin Group (NZ), cnr Airborne and Rosedale Roads, Albany,
Auckland 1310, New Zealand (a division of Pearson New Zealand Ltd.)
Penguin Books (South Africa) (Pty.) Ltd., 24 Sturdee Avenue,
Rosebank, Johannesburg 2196, South Africa

Penguin Books Ltd., Registered Offices:
80 Strand, London WC2R 0RL, England

First published by Signet, an imprint of New American Library,
a division of Penguin Group (USA) Inc.

First Printing, June 2005
10 9 8 7 6 5 4 3 2 1

The first chapter of this book previously appeared in *Colorado Claim Jumpers,* the two hundred eighty-third volume in this series.

Copyright © Penguin Group (USA) Inc., 2005
All rights reserved

 REGISTERED TRADEMARK—MARCA REGISTRADA

Printed in the United States of America

The Trailsman

Beginnings . . . they bend the tree and they mark the man. Skye Fargo was born when he was eighteen. Terror was his midwife, vengeance his first cry. Killing spawned Skye Fargo, ruthless, cold-blooded murder. Out of the acrid smoke of gunpowder still hanging in the air, he rose, cried out a promise never forgotten.

The Trailsman they began to call him all across the West: searcher, scout, hunter, the man who could see where others only looked, his skills for hire but not his soul, the man who lived each day to the fullest, yet trailed each tomorrow. Skye Fargo, the Trailsman, the seeker who could take the wildness of a land and the wanting of a woman and make them his own.

The Dakota Territory, 1861—where blood was thicker than water, and greed was thicker than both.

1

The two roustabouts were going to cause trouble.

They swaggered across the hurricane deck of the *Northern Lights,* bumping into passengers and glaring at anyone who dared comment about their drunken state. The big one was called Finn, his stocky companion was known as Slick, and they were the worst sort of river rats. The kind who would rather loaf than work. The kind who drank on the job, and the captain be damned. The kind who delighted in bullying others.

Skye Fargo saw them come up the main stairway. He stood near one of the *Northern Lights'* smokestacks, unnoticed in the shadows. A big man in his own right, he wore buckskins and a red bandanna and a dusty white hat with the brim pulled low over his lake-blue eyes. Strapped to his waist was a Colt that had seen a lot of use.

Finn and Slick were almost to the jack staff and the woman standing beside it. Amanda Stain did not notice them, or if she did, she did not let on. A stunning brunette, she was the height of fashion in a dress that clung to her shapely figure as if painted on. Her hat fluttered slightly in the breeze, and she held a parasol across one shoulder to ward off the worst of the burning sun.

Fargo was in motion before Finn and Slick stopped. He saw them halt and openly ogle Amanda, saw Finn nudge Slick and grin and walk up to her and say something. It caused her to stiffen but she did not reply. By then Fargo was close enough to overhear.

"I'm talking to you, bitch, and you'd damned well better mind your manners or else."

Amanda turned from the rail and regarded him coldly. "How strange that you of all people should be concerned about proper behavior, Mr. Finn. You are a lout and a lecher, and if you had a shred of decency in your uncouth body, you would not impose yourself on a lady."

Slick snickered and said, "Why, Finn, I don't think she likes you much!"

The roustabout did not like being mocked, any more than he liked being insulted. "You and your airs!" He gripped Amanda's right arm. "You've been looking down your nose at me this whole trip, you and those snotty kin of yours. I have half a mind to slap you silly."

Amanda did not try to break free. She calmly met his lewd gaze and responded, "Persist in this behavior and I will have no choice but to report you to Captain Bettles."

Finn and Slick both laughed, and Slick slapped his thigh and declared, "Go right ahead! For all the good it will do you."

"Our weak-kneed captain doesn't have enough sand to fill a thimble," Finn told her. "We can do whatever we want and get away with it." He leaned closer. "Including having our way with any skirt we take a fancy to."

"Release me this instant," Amanda said.

"And what if I don't?" Finn challenged her.

By then Fargo was there. He did not tap Finn on the shoulder and politely ask the two roustabouts to behave. He did not say anything at all. He simply grabbed Finn by the shoulder, spun him around, and drove his knee into Finn's groin.

Finn doubled over and clutched himself. Staggering

2

against the rail, he turned beet red and tried to say something but all he could do was sputter.

"What the hell?" Slick blurted, rousing to life and clawing for a dagger he wore in a leather sheath on his left hip. "No one does that to my friend!"

Fargo had his Colt out before the weasel could blink and slammed the barrel across Slick's temple. Not once but twice, and on the second blow Slick's knees buckled and he oozed to the deck with spittle dribbling down his chin. Twirling the Colt back into his holster, Fargo turned to the lovely woman they had been abusing. "I can escort you to your cabin if you want."

"Whatever for?" Amanda Stain asked. "You have the situation well in hand, Mr. Fargo. Although I wonder if it was necessary to be quite so violent."

Fargo nudged Slick's unconscious form. "Violence is all men like him ever understand."

"Know that for a fact, do you?" Amanda asked. "Politeness can go a long way if you give it a try."

"It wasn't doing you a damn bit of good, was it? Another minute and they would have ripped off your dress."

Amanda laughed and twirled her parasol. "Honestly, now. In broad daylight? With all these people around?"

Fargo sighed and regarded the other passengers, most of whom had frozen with shock and were standing well back. "These sheep? Finn doesn't care about them. He takes what he wants when he wants it, and he wanted you."

"I still say you overreacted," Amanda insisted, but then her voice softened and she said, "Nonetheless, I thank you for coming to my rescue. Sir Galahad in buckskins. Who would have thought there was such a thing?"

Fargo's estimation of her rose. Before he could respond, there was a commotion at the main stairs, and

Captain Benjamin Bettles and the mate, a bear of a man by the name of Grear, appeared. Bettles was small and thin and had a close-cropped beard that failed to hide the fact he had no chin. His brown eyes nervously flitted from the two roustabouts to Amanda Stain to Fargo.

"I say, sir, what is the meaning of this? Am I to gather you have manhandled two of my crew?"

"Only after they manhandled one of your passengers," Fargo said with a nod at Amanda.

Finn had been on his knees wheezing like a kicked goat, but now he struggled to his feet and growled, "That's a damned lie!"

Fargo's Colt leaped into his hand and he swept it in an arc that caught Finn across the temple and felled him like a poled ox. In the same smooth motion he returned it to his holster and hooked his thumbs in his gun belt.

Captain Bettles was momentarily speechless. Then he cleared his throat and nervously declared, "That was uncalled for. I must insist you turn over that firearm to me. I am confining you to your cabin for the remainder of your stay on board my vessel."

Grear started forward. He had a craggy face split by a jagged scar down the left side. Wedged under his wide leather belt was a Bowie.

"Don't even think it," Fargo warned, dropping his right hand to the Colt.

Grear froze, and Captain Bettles puffed out his cheeks like an angry chipmunk. "See here! I am in command. A captain's word is law, and you will do as I say or I will give the signal and you'll have every hand on board to deal with."

There was only so much Fargo would abide. He disliked Bettles. Not because the steamboat's skipper was weak-willed and let the crew get away with things most captains would not tolerate. Nor because Bettles

4

was incompetent and had run the *Northern Lights* onto sandbars eleven times on their long trip up the Missouri River. No, he disliked Benjamin Bettles because the man was a pompous little jackass. "Go ahead and call your crew," he said, "if you don't mind losing six or seven. And if they don't mind losing their captain."

"You dare threaten *me*?"

Grear was fingering the hilt of his Bowie. "Let me and the roosters deal with him, sir."

Rooster, as Fargo knew, was river slang for roustabout. He was about resigned to having to fight for his life when Amanda Stain stepped up and poked Bettles in his skinny chest.

"That will be quite enough, Captain. Mr. Fargo was only doing what he has been paid to do. Your men, on the other hand, reek of alcohol and were quite insulting. The issue isn't his behavior, it's theirs."

Bettles was too flustered to say anything.

"If you persist with these silly antics," Amanda said harshly, "I will inform my brother of how I was mistreated, and he will inform the owner." She paused masterfully. "This steamboat is owned by Mr. William Kitteredge, of New Orleans, is it not?"

Captain Bettles deflated like a punctured waterskin. "Please, Miss Stain, there is no need to bring the owner into this. I apologize for my crew, and I promise you this will never happen again." He glanced meaningfully at Grear.

Amanda smiled and said sweetly, "Thank you ever so much. I appreciate your sincerity." Then she extended an elbow to Fargo. "I believe I will take you up on your gracious offer. If you would be so kind as to escort me below, I would be ever so grateful."

Fargo waited until they were past the stairs and moving along the passenger compartments to say, "That was some act you put on."

Her green eyes were sparkling. "How else does one deal with idiots? The important thing is I spared you from more violence."

"I didn't know you cared." The warm feel of her arm and the tantalizing fragrance of her expensive perfume set Fargo to imagining how she would look without the dress.

"Don't flatter yourself," Amanda said. "I did it because we need you to get where we're going, and no other reason."

"If you say so." Fargo liked how her lovely face colored pink. "I'm ever so grateful," he mimicked her, and brushed his hand across her fingers.

Amanda said indignantly, "I should slap you. You're no better than those loutish roustabouts."

"But you won't."

"How can you be so sure?" Amanda retorted, and hefted her parasol as if she were thinking of striking him with it.

"You don't like violence, remember?" Fargo gazed past the railing at high bluffs hemming the river and a hawk that wheeled in the sky in search of prey.

"I never said I wouldn't defend my honor if I had to," Amanda said tartly.

"It's not your honor so much as your life you have to worry about," Fargo set her straight. "Dakota Territory isn't New Orleans. Once we're off this boat, we're in Sioux country. In case you haven't heard, they hate whites, and if they catch us, they'll separate you from that pretty hair of yours right before they slit your pretty throat."

"Are you trying to scare me?"

"I'm trying to get you to see that this loco quest your family is on can get all of you killed. Hostiles aren't your only worry. There are bears and buffalo and outlaws, fierce heat and scarce water."

"Goodness gracious," Amanda said lightheartedly.

"Next you'll have me in dread of prairie dogs and grasshoppers."

Fargo should have known better. He had tried to talk her brother out of their hare-brained notion when they approached him in St. Louis, where Thomas Stain had tracked him down. Thomas wanted to hire him for top dollar as a guide. Most men in Fargo's boots would gladly have agreed without a word of warning, but Fargo felt it only fair to give the Stains some idea of what they were in for. They shrugged it off. The whole family was that way. Too much confidence and not enough common sense.

"No comment?" Amanda bantered.

"If you want to get yourselves killed, be my guest," Fargo said testily. In his opinion some people had no business daring the rigors of the wilderness, and the Stain clan were at the top of the list.

"Evidently I have more confidence in your abilities than you do," Amanda said. "You're supposed to be the best there is at what you do. Scout, frontiersman, plainsman, whatever you care to call yourself, you have quite a reputation. My brother learned all about you."

As if on cue, a cabin door opened ahead and out stepped Thomas Stain. Like his sister, he was dressed in the best clothes his wealth could buy. His hat was tilted at a rakish angle, his suit impeccable. In his left hand was a polished cane with an ivory handle. "Sis! Mr. Fargo. I'm on my way to the boiler deck for some fresh air." He swiped at a speck of lint on his sleeve. "I can't stand to be cooped up for very long."

Fargo couldn't either. He preferred the vast prairie, the towering Rockies. Spending weeks inside a cramped compartment was enough to have him hankering after wide open spaces.

"Join me, won't you?" Stain requested, and headed aft without waiting for a reply.

"Your brother takes too much for granted," Fargo said.

"He's accustomed to having others do as he wants," Amanda responded. "He's a leader of men, not a follower."

"Even so, how can you let him drag you and your sisters off into the middle of nowhere?"

"First off, he's not dragging us, it's our mutual decision. Second, people travel across the prairie all the time. Wagon trains go from St. Joe to Oregon and freight trains from Kansas City to Santa Fe. It's a lot safer than you would have us believe."

Why was it, Fargo wondered, that some people always had an answer for everything? He had lived on the frontier nearly all his life. His roaming had taken him from the Mississippi River to the Pacific Ocean, from Canada to Mexico. He had experienced the blistering oven of the southwestern deserts, the bitter cold of snowcapped mountain peaks. He had lived with Indian tribes, tangled with others. Few men, white or red, had seen as much of the frontier as he had, yet here was Amanda Stain, who had never set foot west of New Orleans her whole life long, telling him that they had nothing to worry about.

The boiler deck was not crowded except to starboard where Fargo saw a group of passengers he recognized. There was Charles Stain, older brother to Thomas and Amanda, and their sisters, Elizabeth and Emma. There was William Peel, a distant cousin, whose hair was as oily as his manner. There was Pompey, a black manservant, and Monique, the family maid, a petite, truly beautiful young woman. Finally, there was Maxton, who hovered in the background like a vulture waiting for a feast of carrion.

"It looks like everyone wanted fresh air," Fargo said.

Thomas twirled his cane. "Since we will be disembarking in a few days, I thought it wise to hold this meeting, as it were, to settle any last-minute issues which might be raised."

"I have one," Fargo mentioned. "You still haven't told me where the hell you want to go." All Stain had revealed was that they wanted him to guide them north across the prairie from a certain point on the river. "Why all the secrecy?"

"I have my reasons," Thomas said. "But it won't do any harm to share a bit more information. You see, Mr. Fargo, we want you to find something for us."

When Stain did not go on, Fargo goaded him with, "What, exactly? A lost gold mine? A white buffalo? Wild horses?" At one time or another, he had been hired to find all three.

"No, no." Thomas Stain chuckled. "Nothing so silly, I assure you." He smiled broadly. "We're on a quest to find a ghost town."

2

The *Northern Lights* was one of the new breed of steamboat plying the riverways of the West. A sleek stern-wheeler able to hold over three hundred tons of cargo while drawing only thirty inches of water, her design was such that she should skim over sandbars as though they were not even there. Yet somehow Captain Bettles managed to snag her on two more before the morning was out. Fortunately the crew was able to work her loose without too much effort.

Toward the middle of the afternoon they experienced another delay. As often happened this far up the Missouri, the steamboat was running low on fuel. As a result, Captain Bettles brought her in close to a timbered slope and dropped anchor. A yawl was lowered and men were sent to chop trees.

The passengers were eager to stretch their legs so Bettles gave permission for as many as wanted to venture ashore. They had to wade from the ship to the low bank. Mothers carried children and husbands helped their wives. Once there, they spread out, happy to be on land again, however briefly.

The Stains decided to go, too. Not one of them asked Fargo if he thought it was safe. If they had, he would have told them that nowhere west of the Mississippi River was ever safe, and certainly not a riverbank in the heart of Sioux country. He tagged along, and when Thomas Stain and the other men and the manservant hiked off to the right and the women and the maid hiked to the left, Fargo went left.

The three sisters were having a fine time, chatting and laughing and pointing at birds and wildflowers. Monique hung back, her small hands clasped in front of her, dutifully waiting until she was needed.

Fargo had caught the maid studying him a few times when she thought he wouldn't notice. She was quite an eyeful. Her black hair was cropped close, with bangs that hung down to her eyes. Her uniform would shock a Puritan. Cut low in front to highlight her cleavage, the hem was midway between her hips and her knees. Small wonder she was the object of many a lustful stare from many of the passengers and crew.

Fargo scanned the woods but did not see cause for worry. Odds were the Sioux would not try anything with so many whites about, not when dozens of the passengers had guns.

Amanda, Elizabeth and Emma Stain found a convenient log to sit on. Monique said something, and when Amanda gestured, she turned and walked toward the river.

Fargo shadowed her to a grassy bluff overlooking the Missouri and the *Northern Lights*. She watched roustabouts ferrying wood to the steamboat and then gazed across the river at an equally high bluff on the other side. "It is so beautiful here," she said aloud.

"Is this your first steamboat trip?" Fargo asked.

Monique gave a start, her hand flying to her throat. *"Monsieur!* You gave me quite a scare! I did not hear you come up."

"I didn't mean to spook you," Fargo said. He squatted and plucked a stem of grass and stuck it between his teeth. "A lot worse could happen before this is over."

"Monsieur?" Monique said quizzically, then her an-

11

gelic features brightened and she nodded. "Ah. I think I understand. You warn me, yes, as you warned the Stains? About the dangers?"

"If you're smart you'll refuse to go," Fargo advised. "Whatever they're paying you, it's not enough."

Monique said indignantly, "Excuse me, but you do not decide my life for me. They expect I will go and I can do no less."

Fargo admired how her bosom filled out her uniform, and the enticing swell of her thighs. She was the kind of woman a man would daydream about in his idle moments, and yearn for in the lonely hours of the night. "Do they pay you enough to take an arrow for them?"

"Take an arrow?" Monique repeated. "Oh. I see. But it is not for the money I do this. It is for the paper I signed. The contract."

Her accent gave her voice a delightful lilt. She would sound even better, Fargo reflected, in the throes of passion. "Did that contract provide for your next of kin?"

"Again you try to scare me," Monique said. "But I am not a little girl to be frightened by tales of savage men and wild beasts."

"The Sioux and the Blackfeet aren't savages. They're mad. Mad as hell because whites are slowly driving them off land their peoples have roamed for more moons than the oldest can remember."

"You almost sound as if they have your sympathy," Monique observed. She avoided looking straight at him.

"They do," Fargo said. "So do the Apaches and the Comanches and anyone else who stands up for what is theirs. I don't like all the killing but it's the only way they know to fight back."

"Even so, I will stay with the Stains. I thank you for worrying about me. It is very sweet."

Sweet wasn't enough. Twice now Fargo had tried to talk some sense into them and each time he had failed. "What about Pompey? Is he as devoted to his work as you are?"

"It is not the work, *monsieur,* it is my word. I am *la fille de chambre.* To some this might not be much but to me it is everything." Monique paused. "My English, it is good enough, yes?"

"More than good enough," Fargo assured her. To his surprise, she stepped up to him and placed a hand on his shoulder. That close, her charms were as alluring as ripe fruit; he wanted to reach out and pluck them.

"You really are sweet, *monsieur.* Perhaps we will talk again sometime. I think I would like to get to know you better."

Before Fargo could object she dashed into the woods in the direction of the Stain sisters. Her pert backside had a saucy sway to it that fed a hunger deep inside him. Sighing, he stood and slowly followed. He would make one last appeal to the three sisters, and if that didn't work, whatever befell them was on their shoulders.

Suddenly loud cries broke out to the north, past the steamboat. Cries of "Indians! Indians!" and more, but Fargo could not catch the rest. He ran to find out what was going on, and he was not the only one. Passengers were streaming from all directions. There was nothing like the threat of hostiles to get them agitated.

A crowd already ringed the cause of the ruckus. Fargo shouldered through them and discovered a burly roustabout on his face with arrows bristling from his back and sides like oversized porcupine quills. The man had been chopping wood and probably never saw the warriors who brought him low.

"Let me through, damn it!" someone gruffly bellowed, and Grear, the mate, was there. "It's Harvey! I gave orders that no one was to stray off alone but he didn't listen."

"We should get back to the boat," a passenger urgently suggested. "The heathens must be nearby."

It sparked a general rush to the *Northern Lights*.

Fargo did not join in the panic. Bending low, he examined the ground for sign. Finding none, he scoured the underbrush for likely spots where the warriors had been hidden. A nearby thicket sparked his interest. Behind it, in a patch of bare earth, was a partial moccasin print.

"What have you found?" Grear and half a dozen crewmen armed with rifles and pistols had come up.

Fargo showed him.

"Can you backtrack them?" the ship's mate asked. "If they're still around, we need to know." His anger and resentment of earlier were gone.

Nodding, Fargo stalked into the brush, drawing the Colt as he went. He was sure the culprits were Sioux. No two tribes made their arrows exactly alike, and he had lived among the Sioux long enough to identify their arrows at a glance.

No two tribes made their moccasins exactly alike, either, and Fargo found enough prints and partials to confirm the identity of the four warriors involved. Right after they killed Harvey, they had slipped quietly and quickly away before they were discovered.

By the time Fargo returned to the steamboat, a burial detail was disposing of Harvey's remains under the watchful guns of armed roustabouts on deck.

Captain Bettles was waiting for him. "What did you find?" he impatiently demanded. "How many are there? Dozens? Hundreds? Are we about to be overrun? Speak, man! Speak!"

"All four of them could overrun you anytime now," Fargo said dryly.

"That's all there were?"

Fargo nodded. "They're on their way back to their village to tell how they counted coup on your crewman. I doubt he knew what killed him. On land your men are next to worthless."

Bettles' thin lips pinched together. "I don't like you, mister. Were it up to me, I would leave you here."

"You could try," Fargo said. He pushed past the pathetic excuse for a captain and went aft to check on the Ovaro. Thomas Stain was paying a considerable sum for the privilege of transporting it. Stain had no choice. Fargo refused to use any other horse. As he had put it, "No Ovaro, no me."

Fargo didn't trust the crew to keep the stallion fed and watered, so after the first day on board he informed Stain and Bettles that he would do it himself. Now he used a pitchfork to spread fresh straw in the pen. The stallion nuzzled him and he spent a few minutes keeping it company. It was holding up well, all things considered, but he knew it missed the open country as much as he did.

The burial was soon over and Captain Bettles prepared to get under way. Fargo went forward to his compartment and had the door halfway open before he realized someone was inside. A soft sound gave the intruder away. Instantly, Fargo dived flat, unlimbering the Colt as he dropped.

"My word!" Emma Stain exclaimed. "You're not going to shoot me, are you?" The youngest of the three sisters was seated in the only chair, her hat in her lap. Her hair was lighter than Amanda's and hung in carefully coiffured ringlets. She had the same oval face, the same green eyes, but her lips were fuller.

Feeling slightly foolish, Fargo picked himself up, shoved the Colt into his holster, and closed the compartment door. "How did you get in here?"

Emma smiled and held up a small key, a duplicate of his own. "The captain has a spare set."

"You asked and he gave it to you just like that?" Fargo snapped his fingers.

"A certain sum exchanged hands," Emma said. "Incentive, you might call it."

Fargo sat on the edge of the bunk with one leg crooked under him. "Let me guess. You want a back rub?" Her visit was as puzzling as it was unexpected. Except for Thomas, the Stains had generally avoided him the whole trip. Emma hadn't said ten words to him, yet here she was, putting herself in a situation most young women would regard as compromising.

Laughter bubbled from Emma like water from a fountain. "You can wish that's why I came, but don't flatter yourself. You're not the type of man who ordinarily interests me."

"Oh?" Fargo said.

"My tastes are more refined. Give me a gentleman over a plainsman any day of the week."

"Be careful. All this flattery will go to my head."

Emma showed her white, even teeth in a wide grin. "It's nothing personal, I assure you, and I must say that as plainsmen go you're exceptionally handsome. Both my sisters made mention of that fact."

"Have they, now?" Fargo said. Neither had let on, though, that he was anything other than hired help.

"I'm here because I have a few questions," Emma revealed.

"Questions you had to ask in private?" Fargo didn't know what she was up to but there was more here than met his eye.

"Thomas might misconstrue if he found out, and I'd rather not upset him. He's the leader of our little expedition, even though Charles is older by five years."

"I wondered about that," Fargo mentioned. "Shouldn't it be the other way around?"

"Normally, I suppose. But Charles has always been much too lackadaisical, even as a boy. Tom, on the

16

other hand, loves to take charge and get things done. The family firebrand, you might say."

"How about you? Where do you fit into the scheme of Stain things?"

"Me? I'm the one everyone else tends to ignore. That happens when you're the youngest. Your opinions never count for much. But they are my siblings and I always stick by them through thick and thin." Emma paused. "Which brings me to why I came to see you. I gather from comments you have made that you think we are making a terrible mistake?"

"Dakota Territory is no place for greenhorns," Fargo said.

"By that you mean we are city dwellers and as such we have no business traipsing about the wilderness?"

"You're like fish out of water."

Emma smoothed her dress while thoughtfully regarding him. "Others have crossed this territory. Settlers and the like. Why not us? We'll be well armed. We have more than ample provisions. And Tom hired you as our guide. The best scout in the whole army. What else could we possibly do to satisfy you? If you ask me, my brother has thought of every contingency."

Fargo leaned on his elbows. "I'll get you where you want to go," he promised, even though they had yet to tell him exactly where that was. "But there's only so much I can do. Did you see the dead roustabout today?" When Emma blanched and nodded, he went on. "Sioux killed him. A party of hunters, probably, who saw the steamboat put to shore and couldn't resist. War parties are usually bigger. Think what will happen if we run into one when we're off on this grand adventure of yours."

"It's that serious, then?"

"What do I have to do to get through to you? How long before you believe that everything I've been telling you is true?" Fargo was losing his patience with them, and almost swore. "I don't make a habit of lying, lady. But I'll say it one more time just so I'm sure you understand." He locked eyes with her. "There's a very good chance none of you will make it back alive."

3

Fargo pondered over Emma's visit after she left. She had not said much else, merely thanked him and departed. Which had him wondering what the point had been. Either she thought Thomas was making a mistake and wanted her fears confirmed, or she had a secret reason.

The motion of the *Northern Lights* told him they were under way. Fargo lay back on the small bunk and removed his hat. The corn husk mattress wasn't all that comfortable, but he had slept on worse.

Other than taking another walk on deck, there was nothing much to do. The boredom was getting to him. Day in and day out of the same dull routine. He listened to the throb of the engine, which never stopped even when the craft was at rest, and without meaning to, he dozed off. When next he opened his eyes the compartment was dark. A glance at the window explained why. Twilight had fallen. Annoyed he had slept so long, he sat up and stretched, shoved his hat back on and went out.

A brisk breeze was blowing. Fargo moved forward, shaking off drowsiness, until a sudden snarl brought him up short. He had accidentally stepped on the tail of a scrawny cat. It bolted aft, a furry streak, past a deckhand who bawled, "Come here, you! How did you get out?"

Four large cages full of cats were being shipped to

forts upriver, where they were desperately needed. Rats infested military posts, devouring expensive grain meant for the soldiers and their mounts, and the only way to keep the rodent population in check was with their natural nemesis.

Fargo came to the hurricane deck and stood next to the jack staff. The *Northern Lights* was making good time. Smoke billowed from her twin stacks in great coils, the throb of the deck testifying to the power driving her stern wheel.

Fargo had the hurricane deck to himself. It was the supper hour. The passengers traveling first class, which included the Stain party, were permitted to join the captain in his quarters for their meal. The rest of the passengers, those who had booked passage on the open lower deck and were obliged to supply their own food and sleep unprotected from the elements, were huddled below, partaking of their meager fare.

Fargo wasn't all that hungry. Later he would treat himself to a few pieces of pemmican from a bundle in his saddlebags. For now he was content to rest one foot on the bottom rail and watch the shorelines go by. He spotted several deer, and shortly after, a pair of elk emerged from cover and stared at the monster plying its steady way through their drinking water.

Sticking to the middle of the channel, the steamboat rounded a bend. On the right bank a hulking shape materialized. The wreck of another vessel, one of countless many that had floundered or crashed or capsized braving the turbulent Missouri. This one was charcoal black, with a gaping hole. A clue her boiler had burst, engulfing the boat in flames.

For all its convenience, steamboat travel was extremely perilous.

The sky gradually darkened. Soon Fargo could barely see his hand at arm's length, let alone the shore. Lights came on behind him, lanterns and lamps that were a danger in themselves. All it would take was for one to fall and break and the steamboat would become an inferno.

The sudden scrape of a sole was the only warning Fargo had that someone had snuck up behind him. Whirling, he crouched, and a blade meant for his neck missed. The roustabout wielding it skipped back out of reach. Two others were stalking him from either side.

"Do the captain and the mate know what you're up to, Finn?" Fargo stalled so he could slide his right hand into his right boot and ease his Arkansas Toothpick from its ankle sheath.

Finn smirked and wagged his knife. "We were told to lay off, but Slick and me like to pay our debts, and we brought a friend along for good measure."

"We'll report to the captain that you fell overboard," Slick said. "It happens all the time." He and the other rooster drew knives of their own, and by the way they held them, they knew how to use them.

Fargo was ready. He had the Toothpick out, low against his leg where they couldn't see it.

"Go for your gun, bastard," Finn goaded. "Don't just stand there frozen with fear."

"Jackasses." Fargo could draw and shoot all three before they reached him but the gunfire would bring others, and he preferred to do this quietly.

"Is that so?" Finn said, weaving his knife in a figure eight. "I'll remember you said that as we're dumping you over the side."

They came at him then, three at once, confident and quick and smiling. Fargo's back was to the rail and they thought they had him. But when Finn lanced his blade in high, Fargo went low, opening the roustabout's wrist with a lightning slice. Without breaking stride Fargo pivoted to confront Slick as Slick stabbed at his ribs. Slick's weapon grazed Fargo's buckskin shirt but didn't cut through to the skin. Before Slick could pull back, Fargo sliced his forearm open.

That left the third roustabout, their friend. He

thrust at Fargo's unprotected back but Fargo was expecting it and sidestepped, turning as he moved so that all it took to disarm this one was to slash the Toothpick across the back of his hand, opening his knuckles wide.

"Want more?" Fargo asked. He had spared them so far but only because killing them might cause him more bother than they were worth. Bettles was just the sort to try and throw him in irons even though they had started it.

"Damn right I do!" Finn responded. Large drops of blood were dripping from his wrist but he had switched his knife to his other hand. "You won't be as lucky this time."

From out of the inky veil behind them sprang a solid slab of muscle. Grear had his Bowie in one hand, a short club in the other. A blow from the club crumpled Slick in his tracks. Then Grear had the Bowie against Finn's throat and growled, "The captain told you to let this one be!"

"But we owe him!" Finn protested. "You saw what he did to us!"

"What he did or didn't do is no concern of mine," Grear said. "I serve the captain. I follow his commands, and he sent me to fetch him. So what will it be?" Grear hefted his weapons and waited.

Finn shook with raw fury. "I hate backing down. But your word is law." On a steamboat the mate was the captain's right hand, and crewmen who failed to do as the mate told them were severely punished. "Damn you to hell!" Finn snarled at Fargo, and moved aside.

"Take Slick aft and stitch yourselves up," Grear commanded. "I'll talk to you later." To Fargo he said, "Come along. We don't want to keep Captain Bettles waiting."

Fargo warily sidled past the furious roustabouts. He didn't trust them as far as he could throw their vessel.

"This isn't over," Finn said. "Not by a long shot."

Grear led Fargo up the short stairs to the wheel-house. At his knock, the captain's high-pitched voice bid them enter.

Bettles was at the wheel, concentrating on the stretch of river ahead. "There's a snag on the right I need to watch out for. It punched a hole in the *Far East* last month."

"Why did you want to see me?" Fargo asked. He didn't care for the man's company and didn't care if Bettles knew it.

"In a moment. Despite what you might think of me, I take my responsibilities seriously." Bettles peered out the starboard window with the intensity of a hunting hawk. "The damn thing has to be there somewhere. Do you see it, Mr. Grear?"

"No, sir," the mate responded.

"Captain Forrester was quite specific, and he would never mis—." Bettles suddenly pointed. "There, by God! And we've barely room to spare!" Frantic, he spun the wheel to port.

Fargo saw it, too. A giant tree, uprooted by the elements and sent plunging down a bluff to lie partially submerged at the bluff's base. Any one of several of its large branches were thick enough to smash a hole in the ship's hull. For a few harrowing moments he thought the *Northern Lights* would hit it, but thanks to Bettles' vigilance, the steamboat cleared the tree with a yard to spare.

"You did it!" Grear cried.

Captain Bettles exhaled and smiled and smacked the wheel. "Being a pilot is a thankless task. When I take us safely past hundreds of obstacles, no one notices. But if I happen to run aground a few times, I never hear the end of it."

Fargo had to admit the man seemed to know what he was doing. And their trip so far could have been a lot worse. He recollected hearing about a pilot who grounded a steamboat several hundred times in one trip and took six months to travel what should have taken two.

"Now then," Bettles said, turning. "First, I owe you an apology. I was rude this morning. Can you forgive me?"

"I can try."

"Second, I need your opinion. Mr. Stain tells me you have worked as a scout for the army and you're considered an expert in Indian matters. Is this true?"

"Would Stain lie?" Fargo's estimation of the good captain dropped another notch. Bettles' apology had been about as genuine as a counterfeit bill.

"No, I guess not. In that case, perhaps you will be so good as to render some advice. Is it, or is it not, safe for me to land men ashore at daybreak to gather more wood?"

"You don't have enough?"

"Nowhere near it. Poor Harvey was riddled before we were half done, and we need to stockpile a lot before we reach the next stretch of prairie, which, as you must be aware, is essentially treeless." Bettles paused. "I fear we might run into more redskins. Savages are quite clever in their primitive way. Those Sioux might have sent riders to cut us off."

"That's possible," Fargo allowed.

"Then you can understand my predicament. I don't want to put most of my crew ashore to gather more wood, only to have them wiped out. So, please, what is your best assessment of the situation? Is it safe?"

"As safe as anything in life ever is."

"That's hardly an adequate answer, Mr. Fargo. You must be more specific," Captain Bettles said curtly.

Fargo gave it to him truthfully. "I can't predict what the Sioux will do any more than I can predict the weather. If there's a village near where your man was killed, then yes, a war party might be on its way, cutting across country."

24

"As I dreaded," Captain Bettles said. "I have a favor to ask, then. Since you have fought Indian campaigns, are you willing to lead the wood detail in the morning? I'll place the lives of my men in your hands."

Several of whom, Fargo reflected, just tried to throw him overboard.

"Well?" Bettles urged. "Surely you won't let fellow white men die at the hands of a bunch of stinking, lice-ridden heathens?"

Fargo tried to tell himself that he shouldn't judge all the roustabouts by a few bad apples, and that he shouldn't blame the whole crew for their captain's stupidity. But his mouth formed the word anyway. "No."

"You won't help us?"

"I won't lead the wood party. Give every man a gun and have them post sentries and they'll do fine." Fargo left before Bettles embroiled him in an argument. He was at the bottom of the wheelhouse steps when the door slammed shut.

"Not so fast, mister," Grear said. "You can't walk out on us like that."

"I just did." Fargo started to go around the steps to the forward deck but the mate suddenly vaulted over the rail, blocking his way.

"You're not going anywhere until the captain says you can," Grear informed him, "and he's not through with you yet."

"Yes, he is." Fargo was sick and tired of people telling him what he could and couldn't do.

Grear had replaced the Bowie in its sheath but he still held the short club. "Don't make me use this, mister. Go back up and hear what Captain Bettles has to say and spare yourself a beating."

"That works both ways," Fargo said. He started to go past and nearly had his forehead bashed in. He ducked the mate's next swing barely in time, shifted, and drove his right fist into Grear's gut. It was like

25

hitting a tree. The man had muscles enough for five men.

"I tried to be reasonable," Grear said, and swept the club at Fargo's chin.

Jerking back, Fargo lost his balance and tripped over his own feet. He wound up flat on his back. Before he could rise, Grear was on him, the club streaking at his face. Rolling to the right, Fargo avoided the blow while simultaneously kicking Grear in the legs and knocking them out from under him.

Catching hold of the rail, the mate stayed upright. Fargo lashed out again, kicking harder, and down Grear crashed, cursing viciously.

Fargo pushed onto his knees. The club whipped toward his cheek and he brought up his arm to block it. The pain was excruciating. Ignoring it, he clipped Grear's jaw with a right hook, then followed through with an uppercut that left the mate on his side, unconscious, with blood dribbling from his mouth.

A few seconds more and the door to the wheelhouse opened. "Have you persuaded him yet?" Captain Bettles asked.

Fargo swung over the rail and was up the steps in two bounds. He hit Bettles just once, in the pit of the stomach, and the pilot folded, sputtering and wheezing. Seizing him by the throat, Fargo bent so they were eye-to-eye. "No, he didn't persuade me. And if you ever try that again, there will be hell to pay." He wasn't in the habit of making childish threats but the captain and crew of the *Northern Lights* had pushed him as far as he was willing to be pushed. He shoved Bettles through the open door and against the wheel, then got out of there before he did something that would inconvenience everyone on board.

His blood boiling, Fargo descended to the boiler deck. He remembered to keep an eye out for Finn and Slick. When a pair of roustabouts came out of the dark toward him, he instinctively stabbed for his Colt.

But it was two other crewmen going about their business. They walked right by him without so much as a glance.

Fargo unlocked the door to his compartment and groped along the wall until he found the table and the lamp. Lighting it, he adjusted the wick until the glow suited him. He turned to close the door but someone was in the doorway.

"Don't mind another visit, do you?" Emma Stain asked.

"Twice in one day?" Fargo said. "What did I do to deserve all this attention?"

Emma entered and shut the door behind her. "Nothing yet," she said with a smile, "but I have high hopes."

4

Although there was an old saying to the effect that a man should never look a gift horse in the mouth, Fargo's suspicions were aroused. "What is this? We hardly know each other."

"According to the stories people tell about you, that's never stopped you before," Emma said with an impish grin. "You have a reputation for being extremely fond of the fairer sex."

True, Fargo had to admit, but there was something strange here. Her sudden interest in him was a bit *too* sudden. "What would your brothers and sisters say?"

"They do what they want. I do what I want." Emma frowned. "I'm a little disappointed. When I throw myself at a man, I expect him to welcome me with open arms. Your eagerness leaves a lot to be desired."

"Do this a lot, do you?" Fargo went to the table and opened his saddlebags and took out the bottle of whiskey he had brought along. Liquor was not sold on board so he'd had to nurse it the whole trip, and it was half empty. Opening it, he took a healthy swallow and savored the burning sensation that spread down through his throat to his stomach. "Care for a drink?"

"Don't mind if I do." Emma accepted the bottle. Looking at him defiantly, she tipped it to her lips and swallowed twice, then lowered it and gave it back. She didn't blink or cough or shudder.

"You've done that before," Fargo said.

"Drunk whiskey? Why wouldn't I? I've also had Scotch and rum and brandy and, well, you name it." Emma laughed lightly. "What? Have I just destroyed your image of me as a delicate flower?"

"Something like that." Fargo had no objection to women who liked a jolt of hard liquor now and again. Given his fondness for tonsil varnish, he could hardly cast stones. But something about Emma's unexpected ability to handle it so well bothered him.

"Still that puzzled look in your eyes?" she said a trifle angrily. "Some lady-killer you are. I was hoping that for once a rumor was true."

"So that's what this is about?" Fargo asked. "You're playing some sort of game?"

"I assure you," Emma said. "I never do anything frivolous. I'm here because I thought you might be interested in me but apparently I was mistaken."

Fargo had a decision to make. Not that there was ever any doubt about what it would be. "Have another drink?" he said, offering her the bottle.

"Oh my. Are you trying to get me drunk so you can have your way with me?" Emma enjoyed another healthy chug, and smiled. "It goes down smooth and easy. You know your whiskey. Just as you're supposed to know a lot of things."

"I'm the big expert tonight," Fargo said, thinking of Bettles' summons to the wheelhouse. He sipped more whiskey while stepping to the bunk, and sat on the end with his legs wide apart, facing her. "That's why your brother hired me, isn't it?" he fished for information.

"Tom asked around and was told that you're one of the best scouts on the continent," Emma confirmed. "Daniel Boone and Jim Bridger rolled into one, was how a certain colonel phrased it." She paused. "Why?"

"If I'm half the man he thinks I am, why doesn't

he trust me? I still don't know where you want me to take you, other than that nonsense about a ghost town."

"We have our reasons for not revealing too much, too soon," Emma said. "And why is the ghost town nonsense?"

"There's only one I know of in the whole territory. Pembina, up near the Canadian border. It was settled by folks from Canada before the boundary was set, and when they found out the town was on the U.S. side, they packed up and went back north." As best Fargo could recollect, that had been thirty years ago.

"There is another," Emma said guardedly. "Much smaller and much closer than the Canadian border. It was abandoned within a year of being built, and few know of its existence."

A lot of towns sprang up fast but did not last long, Fargo knew. Mining towns were notorious for withering as soon as the ore that spawned them ran out. Other towns folded for other reasons. A poor choice of sites, as in the case of a town built at the base of a mountain, wiped out by an avalanche. Or towns that ran out of water. Or towns that couldn't lure in enough customers to keep their businesses thriving.

"Who in their right mind starts up a town in the middle of Sioux country?" Fargo asked.

"Someone who thought he was better than they are, who saw himself as meaner than any savage could ever hope to be. Who believed that all it took to teach them to stay away was to kill a few as an example."

Fargo had met enough bigots to know the kind of man she described. "This man built a town and the Sioux wiped him out?"

"So the story goes," Emma said, "but whether it's true or not, we'll find out when we get there."

"*If* we get there. The Sioux don't like whites invading their territory. Or don't you care if you end up scalped or have to spend the rest of your days in a Sioux lodge?"

"Thomas assures me we'll be safe."

"The man who started the ghost town felt he was safe, too, didn't he?" Fargo pointed out.

"You're just trying to scare me," Emma said defensively.

"Damn right I am. I've been trying to scare all of you into using your brains for more than hat racks. I've seen what the Sioux can do. I've seen scalped and mutilated bodies. An old trapper they skinned alive. A soldier they cut into pieces. A woman who choked to death on her—"

"Enough, please!" Emma looked troubled. "Spare me the gory details. Yes, I'm well aware of the danger. We all are."

"Yet you still want to go."

Emma nodded. "People have to do some things in life whether they want to or not. It's the nature of things."

"What's in this ghost town that's so important?"

Emma opened her mouth to answer but closed it again, and smiled. "No, you don't. Tom will be mad if I say too much. He'll tell you when the time is right." She glanced at the door. "Besides, you never know when someone might be eavesdropping."

To hide his disappointment Fargo took another slug of red-eye. He didn't like being kept in the dark.

"You puzzle me," Emma was saying. "Here I practically plant myself in your lap and you would rather talk." She walked to the bed and grinned down at him. "Aren't you the least bit interested?"

"I'm not dead yet," Fargo said. He was more than interested. The swell of her bosom, the alluring hint of nicely shaped thighs under her clinging dress, were enough to give any man ideas a parson would find sinful.

"I see. You want me to take the first step so I can't blame you afterward. Is that how this goes?"

"Put any words in my mouth you like." Fargo leaned to his right and placed the bottle on a small stand. Then, pushing his hat back, he smirked up at her. "I'm all yours, ma'am."

"My, my. Aren't you polite? But I want one thing made clear. No strings are attached. I'm not in love with you. I'm not even sure I like you. But I do like intimacy, and it has been much too long since my last interlude."

"So you elected me?" Fargo laughed. "It's my lucky day."

"Don't be crass. Who else would I pick? One of the deckhands? Not only are they uncouth, they would brag about it at every tavern and saloon they visit for the rest of their lives. And none of the other passengers appeal to me half as much as you do." Emma placed a hand on his knee. "Is there anything I've failed to cover? Do you have it all clear now? I'm a woman with needs. Nothing more, nothing less."

"The heifer wants a bull," Fargo said.

Emma frowned. "I don't know as I like being compared to a cow. How about a ram to my ewe?" When he made no move to reach up to her, her frown deepened. "What in the world is the matter now? You should be drooling at the opportunity."

"I'm trying to figure out what you're up to."

Emma's green eyes narrowed. "Why must I have an ulterior motive? Can't a woman like to make love? Or is that a male prerogative?"

"I've known women who do," Fargo acknowledged. "I've known women who don't. But that's not what this is about. It's about you thinking I'm stupid."

Emma drew back. "Apparently you're more perceptive than I thought. All right. If you must know, I want you on my side when the time comes."

"Your side?"

"That's all I can or will say for now. Other than I might have need of your particular skills later, and this is my not-so-clever way of winning you over." Emma indicated the bed. "I never imagined you would see right through me."

"That's better," Fargo said. "A little honesty goes a long way." He roved his eyes from her lustrous hair to the tips of her polished shoes. "I can't see much with all those clothes you have on."

"You still want to? Even after I've admitted I was using you?" Emma sounded greatly surprised.

Fargo smiled. "You're not using me now." Taking hold of the front of her dress, he pulled her closer, and then with a hard yank brought her down on top of him. She squealed and giggled. They were nose to nose and chest to bosom. Any lingering suspicions Fargo may have had faded.

"Goodness. Once you make up your mind, you don't waste any time, do you?" Emma taunted.

Fargo cupped her bottom and squeezed. Gasping, she arched her back, the pink tip of her tongue sliding out between her ruby red lips. "Is this what you had in mind, Miss Stain?" he asked.

"It's a start," Emma said huskily. She removed her hat and threw it to the floor, then began undoing the tiny buttons at her throat.

Sliding his fingers under the collar, Fargo pretended to be about to rip the dress off.

"No!" Emma shrieked, and pried his fingers loose. "Do you have any idea how much this cost? A little restraint is called for, if you please."

"Just so I know the rules." Fargo molded his lips to hers and her mouth parted to admit his tongue. She groaned deep in her throat. Her hands rose to run through his hair and sculpt the muscles of his shoulders and back.

"Oh, mercy," Emma breathed when they broke for breath. "You should rent a room on Canal Street and charge women by the hour. I predict you would be rich in no time."

Fargo kneaded her backside and she squirmed against him and cooed like a dove. He rolled her on her side to help shed her dress, which took some doing. It had more buttons and stays than any dress he ever saw. "Next time wear a potato sack," he said after they had been at it a while.

Emma laughed and pecked his neck. "Be patient. The reward will be that much more worth the wait."

"It better be." Fargo undid yet another small button.

Suddenly there was a loud knock on the door.

Fargo felt Emma stiffen. Putting a finger to his lips, he quietly rose and went to the lamp and extinguished the flame, plunging the compartment into darkness. The knock was repeated. "Who is it?" he demanded. When there was no answer, he crept over, drew his Colt, and jerked the door open a few inches, standing so no one could see the bunk. "What do you want?"

Charles Stain was at the rail, gazing over the side. "I'm sorry to disturb you, Mr. Fargo," he said cordially, "but I was wondering if you have seen my youngest sister, Emma?"

"You thought she was here?" Fargo rejoined, hoping he sounded suitably annoyed.

"No, but I thought you might perhaps have seen her strolling about on deck. For the life of me, I can't imagine where she has gotten to." Charles seemed to be genuinely concerned.

"It's a big boat. She could be anywhere."

"That's true." Charles noticed the Colt. "My word. Do you always greet people with a revolver in your hand?"

"Better safe than dead." Fargo was anxious to return to Emma. "Is there anything else I can do for you?"

Charles hesitated. He had light brown hair and

green eyes and a body that had gained too many pounds about the middle. "There is one thing. In a few days we'll disembark for the overland phase of our journey. Tom sent men ahead to have horses and supplies waiting."

"That's nice to know," Fargo said. It was the first he had heard of it. "How many men?"

"What? Oh, four, I believe. Maxton's people. What my brother sees in him I will never know."

Fargo had learned more in the past minute than he ever had from Thomas Stain. "They'll be going with us, I take it?"

"As far as I know, yes," Charles said. "But it's not them I wanted to ask you about. It's the horses."

"You've lost me."

"I've only ever been on a horse once in my entire life, and that was when I was ten. I'm not much of a rider. I'm worried I'll fall behind or slow the rest of you up, and I don't want to be a burden. Is it possible to find me a horse that's easy to handle?"

Fargo admired the man's honesty. "I'll do what I can."

"Thank you." Charles smiled. "Thank you most kindly. I hate to be a bother, but I refuse to ask Maxton. He would laugh at me behind my back." Touching his hat, Charles Stain walked off.

Fargo shut and locked the door, relit the lamp and turned. "Nice brother you have there."

"He wouldn't be so nice if he could see me right this instant." Emma Stain was naked.

5

How she undressed so fast, Fargo didn't know. He put his hat on the table, stripped off his gun belt and his boots and his buckskins, and crawled onto the bunk beside her. She smelled of jasmine and a hint of soap.

Emma was looking where most any woman would look, a hungry gleam in her lovely green eyes. Licking her lips as if she were about to partake of a feast, she said, "That stallion of yours and you have something in common, I see."

Fargo was drinking in her beauty. She had superbly shaped breasts that sloped upward invitingly at their tips, both nipples as rigid as tacks. Her belly was flat and smooth. A downy thatch crowned her nether mount, framed by alabaster thighs. Long, sleek legs molded into calves as nice as calves could be.

"Like what you see?" Emma huskily asked.

For his answer, Fargo pulled her to him. She yielded hungrily. Her fingers explored his chest and sides while her legs rubbed back and forth against his. When he pinched a nipple, she groaned and gripped his hair.

"Yessssss. I like that."

Fargo pinched it again, then bent his mouth to her other breast and rolled her nipple between his lips and sucked on it. Her fingernails bit deep into his hip. Cupping her other breast, he squeezed and massaged it while she ground her lower half into him with increasing urgency.

"I like a man who takes his time," Emma whispered, then rimmed his ear with her tongue. "I wish we had more of it."

"Are you in a hurry?" Fargo asked between nips of her nipple.

"No, but if I take too long Tom and Amanda are bound to pester me with questions. They have the misguided notion that since I'm the youngest, I shouldn't breathe without their consent."

"So you want it quick?"

"Quick and hard and rough." Emma ran a finger down along his thigh and across his leg. "That is, if you're up to it." She found what she was after, and softly whistled. "More up to it than most, I'd wager."

"You talk too much," Fargo said. Pushing her onto her back, he cupped her, low down, and she shivered in anticipation. He kissed her cheek, her throat, her mouth. He tugged on her hair. Then he ever so slowly parted her nether lips and ever so slowly inserted a finger into her core. She was wet for him, wet and hot, and at the contact her hips bucked.

"Damn, what you do to me!" Emma said huskily.

Fargo slid a second finger in with the first and wriggled them. Stifling a cry, she wrapped both arms around his neck and clung to him as if she were drowning and he was all that could save her.

"More!" she panted. "I want more."

Her body was hot to the touch, her breath molten. Fargo stroked his fingers out and in, slowly at first, until he had her puffing like a bellows and moving under him in wanton abandon. Then he stroked hard and fast as she liked, his palm grinding her swollen knob with every thrust. She glued her mouth to his and came up off the bed with her body bent backward in a bow.

"Ahhhhhh! Yesssssssss!"

Fargo inhaled a breast, her nipple rigid against his tongue. She gripped his hair so fiercely, he was sure she would tear it out by the roots. He licked a path from her heaving breasts to her throat, then slowly slid his fingers out.

"Do me," Emma breathed. "Do me now."

Spreading her legs, Fargo knelt between them and aligned his member with her womanhood. She was eager to couple and gripped his pole to guide him. Gripped it a little too hard, causing him to wince.

"Sorry. I got carried away." Emma shifted and the deed was done. "Ohhhhhhhh," she groaned. "It feels so nice."

Fargo couldn't talk for the constriction in his throat. He held himself still, savoring the feel of her, the wetness of her tunnel and the softness of her skin.

"Any time you're ready," Emma said.

The rhythm they settled into was as old as humankind, as natural as breathing or walking. Fargo stroked slowly for a while and she matched him, her eyelids fluttering, in the grip of overpowering desire.

Her ankles rose to the small of his back and stayed there. She moaned low and long and stopped only when he kissed her. The corn husk mattress was rough on his knees and crackled as he moved. When he picked up the pace it crackled louder, loud enough to be heard outside, but he couldn't stop if he wanted to and he didn't want to.

Emma thrashed her head from side to side. Her exquisite red lips were drawn back from her teeth in what appeared to be a feral grimace but was a testament to the intensity of her impending release.

Then she was there, and it was all Fargo could do to hold on to her bucking form as she spurted. His own release was not long in coming, and then it was a long, slow fall back to earth with his body tingling in bliss.

Fargo expected Emma to stick around a while yet but she surprised him by rolling off the bed and unsteadily rising. "So soon?"

Her face was red and she was caked with sweat and it was all she could do to stand up straight. "They'll be wondering."

"Let them," Fargo said, but she did not crawl back in with him. Weary to the bone, he closed his eyes, and when next he opened them, she was buttoning the last of the tiny buttons on the front of her dress.

"I thank you, kind sir." Emma smiled and fluffed at her hair, then reclaimed her hat and moved to the door. "Remember. I was never here. We never did this."

"For something I never did, it sure was worth doing," Fargo grinned.

"I can count on you then?" Emma asked.

"To keep my mouth shut? Sure." Fargo was on the verge of drifting off. He barely heard what she said next.

"Not that. Can I count on you to side with me when the time comes? I'll make it well worth your while. Consider this an advance." Emma unlocked the door and peeked out. "The coast is clear. Until tomorrow, lover."

"Until tomorrow," Fargo heard himself mumble. Then sleep claimed him and he was adrift in a chaotic jumble of dreams and blackness. At one point he imagined that he looked up and Amanda Stain was staring down at him and shaking her head. Suddenly a sound snapped him awake. He sat up, his mind befuddled, unsure what the sound had been, and was startled to see the compartment door ajar. Belatedly, he remembered that he had not locked it when Emma left, an oversight that could get him killed.

Sliding off the bed, Fargo padded over and peered out. It was the middle of the night and there wasn't a soul in sight. Closing the door, he debated going back to bed. But now that he was up, he felt alert and refreshed. And, too, he liked to prowl the decks at night and have them all to himself. He dressed and pulled on his boots and strapped on the Colt.

The wind was stronger than it had been all day and carried with it a trace of moisture. Fargo walked aft to check on the Ovaro, then climbed to the boiler deck. He passed several roustabouts sprawled behind stacked freight, and in other crannies. The crew did not have their own compartments. They slept where they could, and if the weather turned foul, that was too bad.

To stern were a row of crates containing farm machinery: plows and harrows. Fargo expected to find a sleeping rooster or three but the crates were too exposed to the wind for their liking. There was a narrow space between the crates and the rail where he could be all by himself, and he stood watching the great paddle wheel churn.

The paddle wheel was huge. Twenty-four feet wide and close to twenty feet around, it took two engines to drive it. Someone once told him that the wheel turned twenty times a minute. It turned so fast there was a constant swish of cascading water.

Presently Fargo heard low voices. He turned and peered between two of the crates and saw a pair of shadowy shapes crossing the deck. He thought maybe they were on their way to the toilets, which were aft, above the rudder, but then several more shapes materialized, all moving toward the stern. Drawing the Colt, he crouched low.

Shoes scuffed the deck, and someone angrily asked, "All right. What the hell is so damned important you had to wake us up in the middle of the night and drag us all the way back here?"

"We can talk in private here," said another voice, one Fargo recognized. It was Finn.

"Talk about what?" That sounded like Slick.

"About that fancy pants, Stain, and his family. They were in his compartment earlier, chatting up a storm, and they made the mistake of leaving the door open to let air in," Finn related. "I happened by and heard some of what they said."

"So?" demanded a voice Fargo could not place.

"So they're on their way to a ghost town somewhere north of the Missouri River," Finn said. "That bastard Fargo is their guide."

"Him!" Slick spat. "I've never wanted to stick a knife into someone as much as I want to stick a knife into him. But what does any of this have to do with us?"

"Are you as tired of breaking your back for nothing as I am?" Finn asked. "Wouldn't you like to have some money, for once? Lots and lots of money?"

"Talk sense," another roustabout said.

"Stain and his people are after something. Something valuable. Something worth millions of dollars."

"Millions?" Slick said.

"What is it?" another asked.

"I don't know," Finn answered. "They never came right out and said. All I know is that they think they have a good chance of finding it, and when they do, they'll have more money than they'll know what to do with."

"Sounds half-baked to me. What good does it do us?"

"Think, you idiot. What if we follow them? What if we wait for them to find whatever it is, and then help ourselves? What if *we* end up with the millions instead of them?"

"North, you said?" From Slick. "That's deep in Sioux country. If they catch us we're goners."

"We'll steal rifles from the ship's storeroom," Finn proposed. "With them the five of us can hold off a good-sized war party."

"You're forgetting something," Slick said. "Stain arranged for horses and supplies, I bet. How are we to keep up if we're on foot?"

"That's the good part. I heard one of the Stains say that they're getting off at Foy's Landing. Foy always has extra horses. He trades them with the Sioux for guns and the like, and in return, they don't lift his hair."

"So we steal rifles and buy our own horses and follow them to the treasure, whatever it is?" one of the roosters summed up the plan.

"Then help ourselves," Finn reiterated.

"They're not likely to let us have it without a fight," a roustabout noted.

"So? If we take them by surprise, they'll be dead before they can get off a shot." Finn had an answer for every objection.

"Three of them are women."

"Since when has that made a difference? Have you gotten squeamish all of a sudden?"

"No. But killing men is one thing—killing women is another. We'll be hunted down and have our necks stretched. I can do without that, thank you very much."

"Use your head, Parkins," Finn snapped. "How will anyone know we did it if all the witnesses are dead? We'll bury the bodies so no one ever finds them, and that will be that."

"You can't be sure," Parkins said.

"Aren't you forgetting the Sioux? No one else would be dumb enough to traipse off into their territory. Even if someone did, and even if by some fluke they found the bodies, they'll blame the Sioux, not us."

"It could work," Slick commented.

"Of course it will work!" Finn declared. "I need to know if all of you are with me or not, and if you are, I have an idea how we can learn more." There was a pause. Two of the men said they were in. The others must have nodded. "All right. Here it is. At dawn the captain is stopping to take on more wood. He'll let the passengers go ashore, like before. Some of the Stains are bound to get off. I say we grab one and force him or her to tell us exactly what it is that they're after."

"We won't have much time," Slick said, "and it will be tricky slipping away from the wood detail."

"Leave that to me," Finn said. "As for the other, there's nothing like a sharp blade against a person's throat to loosen their tongue."

"You'll have to kill whoever it is so they can't talk," a conspirator said. "That will bring the captain into it. He'll have Grear snoop around."

"Not if the murderers are as plain as the nose on your face." Finn chuckled. "I saved two of the arrows we dug out of Harvey. After I'm done, I'll plant the arrows by the body. The captain will blame the red-skins. Neat and tidy, eh?"

"You have it all thought out," Slick complimented him.

"Told you. Now back to sleep, and not a word of this to anyone, you hear? Why divide the millions more than five ways?"

"There's just one thing," someone said. "What about Fargo?"

"What about him?" Finn angrily asked.

"I've heard stories. He's scouted for the army. Been everywhere, done everything. They say he's tough, mighty tough."

"Leave Fargo to me," Finn said. "I'll take care of him when the times comes."

"Just so it's after he finds the ghost town," Slick said. "From the sound of things, without him there won't be any millions."

Finn grunted. "If there's nothing else, let's go. Remember, not a damn word to anyone else."

Fargo watched their shadows recede into the darkness. He considered going to Bettles but it would be his word against theirs, and the captain had a habit of always siding with the crew. He didn't trust Grear much, either. The Stains should be warned. Or should they? After all, they had not seen fit to confide in him, and he did not like being used.

What should he do?

6

"You want to do what?" Captain Bettles asked in disbelief.

"I want to lead the wood party," Fargo repeated himself. It was half an hour after dawn and the *Northern Lights* was at rest close to a thickly forested shore. The roustabouts and many of the passengers were gathered on the main deck and Bettles was about to give his final instructions.

Bettles glanced at Grear and then stared quizzically at Fargo. "I don't understand. Last night when I wanted you to do it, you steadfastly refused, even going so far as to assault us."

"You're the one who sicced your mate on me," Fargo reminded him.

"Let's not quibble. Water under the bridge, and all that. But I am curious. Why have you changed your mind?"

"I like it to be my idea." Fargo's reason was no real reason at all but he couldn't reveal the truth. "Put me in charge and you'll have all the wood you need within the hour."

"That's fine. But what about the Sioux? Shouldn't you scout around first to be sure we're not walking into an ambush?"

"Just what I had in mind."

Bettles raised his arms for silence. Once everyone

quieted, he announced that Fargo was in charge of the wood detail, and that an order from Fargo was to be considered an order from him. That last, for the benefit of the crew, brought scowls to the faces of Finn and Slick. Their scowls deepened when Fargo said that he was going ashore to check for hostiles and he wanted a couple of crewmen to come along. Then he pointed at them.

The steamboat was close enough to a low bank that a plank had been lowered. Fargo went across first, taking his Henry rifle. He didn't wait for the two roustabouts. Plunging into the undergrowth, he moved briskly inland. They came on fast behind him, making more noise than a herd of buffalo.

"Wait up, damn you!" Finn rasped.

Instead, Fargo went faster. Soon he was out of their sight. Angling left into a stand of cottonwoods, he crouched. The woods were quiet except for the racket raised by the twosome struggling to catch up to him. If any Sioux were lurking nearby, they would hear and investigate. But none did.

Fargo strained his senses to their fullest and was convinced Bettles' fears about a war party had been unfounded.

Finn and Slick toiled into view. They were armed with Ballard single-shot rifles. Finn also had his long-bladed knife, Slick his double-edged dagger.

"Where the hell is he?" Finn snapped. "We're supposed to help him look around but he goes and leaves us."

"I don't like it," Slick said, his face damp with sweat. "Why did he pick us, of all people? After the hard time we gave him?"

"Who the hell cares? The jackass has played right into our hands. We can turn him into worm food and blame it on the Sioux." Finn grinned and patted the long coat he wore.

"I tell you something isn't right," Slick insisted.

"Aren't you forgetting the Stains need him to find whatever they are after?"

"You're worse than an old woman," Finn scoffed. "Just act friendly. All I want is to beat on him some."

"It's smarter to go back." Slick would not let it drop.

They passed the cottonwoods. Fargo rose from concealment and trained the Henry on their backs. "It was smart to go back but it's too late. Drop those rifles and hold your arms out from your sides."

Finn and Slick spun. Finn started to raise the Ballard but hissed like a snake and let the muzzle drop. "What the hell is this? We're on your side, remember? Why disarm us? What if savages jump us?"

"The rifles," Fargo said, motioning. "On the ground."

Slick complied but Finn balked. His brow was knit in confusion and he kept shifting his weight from one foot to the other. "Say something, damn it! What is this all about?"

"It's about the ghost town, and you following us there. It's about the Stains, and you not killing them." Fargo indulged in a grim smile. "It's about me not wanting you to beat on me." He centered the Henry on Finn's chest. "Last chance."

"I don't know what you're babbling about," Finn glibly lied, but he let go of his rifle and hiked his hands.

"Take five steps back," Fargo instructed them, and when they obeyed, he picked up their rifles, backed off twenty feet, and set them down again.

"What in God's name are you up to?" Finn demanded.

Slick was the sharper of the pair. "Don't you get it? He knows about your plan to steal from the Stains."

Finn blinked. "That can't be. And even if he does, so what? If he shoots us, the captain will have him charged with murder."

"Who said anything about shooting you?" Fargo set down the Henry and drew his Arkansas Toothpick.

For all of five seconds neither roustabout moved. Then Finn slowly lowered his arms and drew his belt knife. "You against the two of us, is that it? With blades?" He snorted and winked at Slick. "Talk about dumber than a stump."

"You have one way out," Fargo told them. "Forget about the Stains and the ghost town and go upriver with the steamboat when it drops us off at Foy's Landing. The choice is yours."

"Let me see if I've got this straight," Finn said, grinning devilishly. "We kill you and have a crack at a million dollars, or we let you live and go on breaking our backs for a living? You call that a choice?"

"I don't like it, Finn," Slick said. "He's too damn sure of himself. We're good with blades, sure, but last time he cut both of us, remember?"

"It was luck. This time we're ready for him. There's no way he can take both of us," Finn boasted. "No way at all." He bent at the knees and extended his knife arm. "Go wide on that side. I'll take this one."

Fargo sidled to the right a few feet, and stopped. The river rats cautiously converged, their steel glittering in the bright morning sun. Finn was grinning in bloodthirsty anticipation. Slick wasn't as confident, and came in much more slowly.

"I'm really looking forward to this," Finn crowed. "It took six stitches to sew up my wrist and it's been hurting like hell ever since."

"A man plays with knives, he should know how to use them," Fargo said.

"Funny. Real funny."

Then there was no more talking. Finn was first to attack, springing in close with his knife sweeping in a vicious arc that would have opened Fargo's jugular had it connected. But Fargo sprang back, pivoting as he did to meet Slick's rush. The stocky roustabout lanced his dagger at Fargo's ribs. Fargo parried with the Toothpick. Steel rang on steel, and at the instant of contact, Fargo sliced downward.

Slick's dagger did not have a guard between the blade and the hilt. He tried to jerk his hand back but he reacted too late. A shriek tore from his throat as the Toothpick sheared through two of his fingers. They plopped to the ground, their stumps spurting blood, and Slick blanched and staggered, pressing his hand to his shirt.

"Did you see? Did you see what he's done?"

"Bastard!" Finn fumed. Rage drove him berserk. He threw himself at Fargo, stabbing, thrusting, swinging, raining frenzied strokes that Fargo barely dodged, ducked or blocked.

Fargo was forced back. He dared not look behind him, dared not take his eyes off Finn. As a result he was taken unawares when his left foot came down on something that rolled out from under him, throwing him off-balance. He had inadvertently stepped on one of the Ballard rifles. Before he could recover, Finn swung again, and although he brought up the Toothpick in time to counter the blow, the force sent him toppling.

Fargo hit on his shoulders and rolled as he landed. As he rose he ripped a handful of grass out by the roots. Finn snarled and pounced, stabbing at Fargo's throat. Skipping aside, Fargo flung the grass in Finn's face. The roustabout instinctively recoiled. For a moment Finn's guard was down, and it was all Fargo needed. He sank the Toothpick to the hilt in Finn's belly and wrenched it out again.

Blood sprayed in a fine mist. Finn clutched at the wound but could not staunch the flow. Whining, he fell to his knees.

Fargo swung toward Slick.

The stocky rooster was pale but had shaken off the shock of losing his fingers. He closed in again, a new-found fire in his dark eyes. Slick had switched the dagger to his other hand but he was not as dexterous with his left as with his right. His thrust was clumsy and exposed his left side.

Slick stepped back and looked down at the hole Fargo's Toothpick had made. He uttered a gurgling sound that ended with dark blood seeping from both corners of his mouth. "I knew it," he said. Then his eyes rolled back in his head and he keeled over.

Fargo swung around again but he need not have worried. Finn was on his face in a spreading red pool, dead. Rolling him over, Fargo unbuttoned Finn's coat. The two arrows were tucked under the river rat's belt. One had broken when he fell but Fargo could still use the half with the barbed point. He drove it into Finn's stomach, into the hole the Toothpick had made, and left it there. The other arrow he shoved into the hole in Slick's side.

Stepping back, Fargo wiped the Toothpick clean on the grass, then surveyed his grisly handiwork. Unless the wounds were examined closely, no one would suspect the Sioux weren't to blame.

Fargo walked to the rifles and picked up a Ballard. Throwing back his head, he yipped like a Sioux warrior and fired the Ballard into the air. He repeated his little act with the other Ballard. Then, after placing one near Finn and the other near Slick, he retrieved his Henry and banged five shots into the ground. That should do it, he decided.

Fargo took his sweet time returning to the *Northern Lights*. Everyone was on deck, at the rail, anxiously waiting. As he strode out of the forest, Captain Bettles and Grear came across the plank to meet him, both holding revolvers.

"What was all that shooting?" Bettles demanded. "Where are Finn and Slick?"

"Dead," Fargo said.

"We heard the Sioux," Bettles said. "How many were there? Are they still out there?"

"It's safe to chop wood," Fargo hedged. "Post armed lookouts, though, and don't let your passengers go into the woods without an armed escort."

Grear asked suspiciously, "How is it the redskins didn't kill you?"

Fargo patted the Henry. "The Sioux haven't seen many repeaters." Which was true as far it went. Most rifles were single-shot.

"You still haven't said how many there were," Captain Bettles noted. "For all I know, half the Sioux nation is out there."

"Have you ever tried to count Indians in the brush?" was Fargo's response. "You better get the wood in fast or the Sioux might spring a surprise on you."

That did it. Bettles hurried onto the steamboat and bellowed orders like a general. Crewmen streamed onto shore to do his bidding, many with axes, nearly all with either a rifle or a pistol. Then came the passengers, those brave enough. They had been told to stay in groups of four or more, with one rifle for each group. The Stains were next to last off, Thomas and Charles in the lead, then the sisters, then their cousin William Peel, and Maxton. Pompey and Monique were left on board.

Fargo smiled at Amanda, Elizabeth and Emma as they went by. Amanda condescended to nod but Emma ignored him. Elizabeth, on the other hand, bestowed a beaming smile, which was strange in light of the fact they had not spent two seconds together since they met.

William Peel detached himself from his relatives and came over, dislike plainly written on his face. A bowler crowned his oily hair, a silver watch chain dangled from his vest. "Might I have a word with you?" he formally asked.

51

"That's seven already."

"What? Oh." Peel smiled thinly. "Tom has asked me to inform you that we will be disembarking at a place called Foy's Landing. Have you ever heard of it?"

"Heard of it, and been there." Twice before, that Fargo recalled. Neither visit impressed him. Oscar Foy was a two-legged sidewinder who had long been suspected of selling guns to hostiles, but so far the army had not been able to catch him at it.

"We should be there the day after tomorrow," Peel said. "From there on, we'll be entirely in your hands."

"Don't sound so happy."

"Let's be frank, Mr. Fargo," Peel said. "I never saw the need to hire you. We are perfectly capable of getting where we need to go without you. But Tom insisted. He thinks your knowledge of this country and the savages is invaluable."

"You don't?"

"I can read a compass as good as the next person, and primitives with arrows hardly frighten me. It boils down to what can you do that we can't?"

Fargo did not let him off the hook that easily. "Is that why you don't like me? Or is there more?"

"My relatives and I have a lot at stake in this venture. You are a complication, and I believe in keeping complications to a minimum." William Peel grinned an oily grin. "Nothing personal, you understand." He strolled off after the others.

The *thwack* of axes biting into trees broke the stillness. A few at first, then more and more until the woods resounded with a continual chorus.

After a while Grear and four crewmen came out of the forest carrying the bodies of Finn and Slick. One crewman was sent to fetch shovels. Grear chose a knoll forty yards downriver as the grave site.

Fargo was watching them dig when Captain Bettles scuttled along the plank, his usual aloof manner gone.

52

"I wanted to thank you for your help. I realize we've had our differences but I'm willing to admit when I was wrong about someone. Too bad about Finn and Slick but it couldn't be helped."

"It sure couldn't," Fargo agreed.

7

Foy's Landing consisted of a dock, a dugout, a log trading post and a corral, on the north shore of the Missouri. The dock was barely deserving of the name, it was so poorly constructed, but somehow it held together and was used by nearly every vessel that plied the river. The dugout served as Oscar Foy's living quarters. Fargo had never been inside, which was just as well. The odors that wafted from the dark opening were enough to churn the strongest of stomachs. The trading post was sturdy enough but there were gaps between the logs and the roof was made of sod in bad need of being replaced.

The corral was three times the size one would expect, built to accommodate the large number of horses Foy always had on hand for trade or sale downriver. Horses, rumor had it, he acquired from the Sioux and other hostile tribes in return for items it was illegal to sell or trade to them.

But a little thing like the law never stopped Foy. A great bear of a man, he wore a shirt made of crudely stitched beaver fur and pants of elk hide. He favored moccasins rather than boots, and was never seen without a brace of pistols and a butcher knife at his waist. His face would never put women into swoons of rapture; thick, beetling brows crowned dark, piglet eyes, and he had no forehead to speak of. Short crinkly brown hair ended within a fraction of his brows. His nose was long and broad, his chin long and pointed. His mouth was a slit that never smiled, never grinned. He had a reputation for always being fair in his dealings with white and red alike, which in part accounted for his being able to survive where no other white man could. He also had a reputation for being unspeakably vicious when provoked.

A story had it that once several men stopped at the landing and had a little too much to drink. For fun they shot into the dugout and one of them climbed onto the trading post to see if the sod could be set on fire. Foy emptied a revolver into the arsonist, wounded all of the man's companions, then took an axe to them and finished the job in spectacularly gory fashion.

All this filtered through Fargo's mind as the *Northern Lights* neared the dock early on an overcast morning. A slate gray sky threatened rain before the day was done.

Captain Bettles brought the steamboat in and announced he would lay over for three hours to take on provisions and to give the passengers another opportunity to stretch their legs.

The Stains were set to disembark. All their personal effects had been piled on the main deck by Pompey and Monique. Thomas and Charles and William were in suits, the sisters in expensive dresses. Maxton hovered in the background, his hand always on the butt of a revolver.

Fargo kept to himself. He had saddled the Ovaro and was holding the reins. From under his hat brim he watched the crew closely. Three of them had been with Finn and Slick the other night and might entertain the notion of sticking to Finn's plan of following the Stains off across the prairie. But Fargo did not know which three they were. None showed the least interest in the Stains except for lustful glances at Amanda, Elizabeth and Emma from time to time.

The *Northern Lights* had dropped anchor and the

plank was being lowered. Soon Bettles gave the word that those who wanted could go ashore.

Fargo was near the front of the line. He led the Ovaro along the dock, careful its hooves did not step in any of the cracks, and over to a hitch rail in front of the trading post. A small sign above the door read, TRADEING POSTE. He wondered if anyone had ever mentioned the misspelled words to Oscar Foy.

The post was long and low-ceilinged and crammed with trade goods. A lot of it Foy obtained as salvage from wrecks. There was everything from Saratoga chips to guns, from snuff to canned goods. Fargo was surprised to find no one inside. He went back out and saw Foy coming from the direction of the corral.

To the right of the corral loitered four men. They were dressed in city clothes and well armed.

Foy greeted Captain Bettles warmly. A habit on Foy's part, and a smart one, since much of his livelihood depended on the steamboat trade.

The Stains had come ashore, leaving it to Pompey and Monique to bring their valises and trunks. Maxton joined the four city men by the corral and shook each of their hands. Something was said that caused all four to glance at Fargo but he pretended not to notice.

Soon the landing bustled with people. Foy and Captain Bettles went into the trading post. So did as many passengers as could fit inside.

Fargo stayed outside. He had all he needed in his saddlebags. Folding his arms, he leaned against the rail. From here on out he could not predict what would happen and he had to be ready for anything.

Thomas and Charles Stain came over.

"I need your opinion, Mr. Fargo," Thomas said. "Is it better to start today or stay overnight and leave in the morning? I only ask because I want to go today and Maxton insists we rest tonight and start fresh. Does it make much of a difference?"

No, it did not, Fargo reflected. Maxton must have a reason for wanting to stay longer and it would be nice to know what that reason was. "You might want your sisters to take it easy one night. From here on out it will get rough."

"I didn't think of that. We will be spending a lot of time in the saddle, won't we?"

Fargo nodded.

"Very well. We'll stay one night. I'll tell the others."

Charles lingered, and when his brother had gone in, he said quietly, "May I speak frankly?"

"I wouldn't have it any other way," Fargo said.

Charles gazed toward the corral. "Please keep a close eye on my sisters. I don't entirely trust Mr. Maxton, and those four hirelings he arranged to meet don't inspire much confidence."

"Why are you doing this?" Fargo asked.

"Confiding in you? Because you're the only one I can rely on."

"No, I meant why are you taking part in whatever your brother is up to? You don't want to be here. I can tell."

"I'm a Stain, Mr. Fargo. I love my brother and sisters and I will stick by them even when I think they are wrong." Charles sighed. "We never should have left New Orleans, never been talked into this insane venture. I blame William and his glib tongue. He's always been able to talk my brother into things."

This was news. "I thought Tom was in charge."

"Oh, he is. Tom is always in charge. That's just how he is. But it was William who came to us with a crazy tale and offered proof the tale was true. Tom and Amanda were keen to go right away. They've always liked excitement and adventure. Me, I would rather spend my days reading and my evenings at the theater.

"This"—Charles motioned at the wilds around them—"is not my cup of tea."

"Want my advice? Turn around and get back on that boat."

"Would that I could, Mr. Fargo. Would that I could. But I'm afraid I can't desert my siblings." Charles gestured. "I know, I know. It might be the death of me. But if a man doesn't stand by his family, he's not much of a man." The oldest Stain touched his hat and went into the trading post.

Fargo wished Charles had listened. The man was too honorable for his own good. In civilized society little harm could come of it, but out here, where no one was as they seemed and a bullet or an arrow in the back was a more common way to die than old age, too much honor *could* be the death of him.

No sooner had Charles disappeared than Maxton and his four underlings came across the clearing. Maxton was smiling, which was a first for him. "I thought maybe we should talk."

"I was wondering when you would get around to it."

"Just like you're wondering about my part in things?" Maxton asked. "Mr. Stain—Thomas, that is—hired me and my friends to look after his party. We're not scouts, like you. We're protectors, you might say."

"Hired guns," Fargo said.

"Oh, more than that. You see, I run a protection service in New Orleans. I protect businesses from scoundrels who might give them trouble. These men here work for me, and they're good at what they do."

Fargo had heard of these "protection outfits." A better description was extortion racket. Businesses had to pay a lot of money for the privilege of being "protected" whether they wanted to pay or not. Some states had passed laws curbing the practice, but the laws were rarely enforced.

"What I'm saying is that we know our place," Maxton had gone on. "We're not out to cause you problems. We're city boys. We know our limitations. Tell us what to do and we'll do it."

It was Fargo's day for agreeable people. "How is it Stain hired you?"

"He knew about me from certain business connections. We're his insurance, you might say, that he'll make it back alive."

Fargo smothered a frown. They were fools. They thought they were tough. They were used to scaring people and had probably busted a few heads along the way. They thought they were a match for warriors like the Sioux but they were deluding themselves. The city was their element. On the frontier they were fish out of water.

"I'm trying to be friendly," Maxton said when Fargo offered no comment. "I'm trying to show you that you can count on me and my boys."

"I'm obliged," Fargo said. But the truth was, he couldn't count on them. For all their bluster, they would break and run if worse came to worst. It never failed.

"Remember. Anything we can do, just say the word." Maxton and his underlings headed for the steamboat.

Fargo drifted to the corral. Of the dozens of horses milling about, he would warrant less than six had ever been saddle-broke. As he leaned on the top rail a rank odor nearly made him gag. Without turning his head he said, "Oscar Foy."

"I thought I recognized you, Fargo." The trader looked him up and down. "It's been a spell since your last visit."

"You're still here," Fargo said. "I guess what folks say is true. There is no justice in the world."

Foy's piglet eyes glittered. "I see your tongue is as sharp as ever. But I don't hold it against you."

"You're all heart."

"I'm all curiosity at the moment. What's with that Stain character and his kin? I hear tell they're headin' north into the middle of nowhere, and you've hired on as their guide. What the hell is out there that could interest a bunch like that?"

"Ask them," Fargo said.

"I did. But they clammed up. Which was strange, considerin' how friendly they were until then. Sort of makes a gent wonder."

"Just so you don't wonder too hard. Stick to trading guns for horses and you should live a few years yet."

Foy snorted. "I didn't know you cared. But it's their funeral. Or haven't you heard? Broken Horn has been actin' up again. He tangled with an army patrol a few weeks back and killed three troopers."

No, Fargo hadn't heard. Broken Horn was a young Sioux warrior eager to prove himself, and the way a young Sioux proved himself was by counting coup. The more coup, the more respect he earned from his people. "Have you traded any guns to him lately?"

"Me?" Foy said in mock dismay. "I only trade guns to Indians I can trust. That young buck would like as not shoot me down. Besides, I wouldn't know how to contact him."

"My boots are turning brown," Fargo said.

"What?" Foy glanced down. "Oh. Good one. Only you could tell a man he's full of shit and make it sound like a compliment." He started to turn away.

"Don't get any ideas," Fargo said.

"About what?"

"I know you, Foy. I know how you think. Leave them alone. It will cost you more than you count on. Maybe your life."

"There you go again," Foy said. "Keep this up and I'm liable to think you want to take me for your wife." He made for the trading post.

The situation was becoming more complicated by the minute. Fargo waited until Foy went in, then he walked around to the back of the corral and studied the soil for sign. There was plenty, and it told him plenty, but he kept the information to himself for the time being.

Passengers were strolling along the bank, the women smiling, the children skipping about and laughing. Roustabouts were lounging at ease, indulging in rare idle moments. Grear was at the dock, standing guard on the steamboat.

When Fargo was sure no one was watching him, he darted behind the trading post. Close to the back door were tracks made as recently as that morning. After examining them, he drifted to the south side of the cabin and a dirty window.

The trading post was jammed. Oscar Foy was at the counter, taking money for a purchase. The Stains were by the canned goods. Other passengers were selecting items or lined up to buy.

Fargo couldn't say what made him suddenly step to the right and whirl. Maybe it was instinct. Maybe it was a whisper of movement his senses registered even though he was not conscious of it. But the step saved his life. The knife thrust at his back missed.

The roustabout wielding it sprang back and crouched. "Thought I had you for sure, you son of a bitch!"

Fargo had never seen the man before. He wondered if it was one of the men from the other night. "Are you loco?"

"Finn and Slick were friends of mine."

"So?"

"So I had a good look at their bodies."

Fargo slid to the right and the man flicked the knife at him. "You should be mad at the Sioux, not me."

"Sioux, my ass! It wasn't Injuns who killed them! It was you!" The roustabout was livid.

"No one else thinks so," Fargo stalled.

"You might have pulled the wool over their eyes, mister, but not mine. I'm going to carve you up and send you down to hell to keep Finn and Slick company."

8

Skye Fargo was fond of poker. He liked the challenge. He liked to call another player's bluff and see the look on his face when he raked in the pot. He did a lot of bluffing himself, when his hand called for it, and he bluffed now. Fargo did not want to kill the roustabout. The man was only avenging his friends. So instead of shooting him where he stood, Fargo drew his Colt, cocked the hammer and said, "I would think twice were I you."

"Go ahead!" the crewman defiantly urged. "Maybe your first shot will get me, maybe it won't. But I promise I'll stick you one way or the other."

"Are you a sawbones?" Fargo asked.

Confusion etched the man's features. "What the hell kind of question is that? I'm no doctor and you know it."

"Then what makes you think I killed Finn and Slick?" Fargo spoke calmly, reasonably, making no sudden moves.

"Finn said you weren't to be trusted, and those wounds didn't look right."

"Seen a lot of people killed by arrows, have you?" Fargo asked.

"Well, no, only Harvey," the roustabout admitted. "But it didn't look right."

"That's why you're doing this?" Fargo took a gamble. He twirled the Colt into his holster. "If you really believe I did it, then go ahead."

"Is this some kind of trick?" the man demanded, slowly straightening. "Sure, it could have been those lousy redskins. Some of the men say they heard war cries but I was helping with the boiler and didn't hear a thing."

Fargo had him. He smiled and said, "If your friends heard war cries, why don't you believe them?"

The rooster sheathed his knife. "All right. I'm makin' a fool of myself. Sorry, mister. No hard feelings?"

"I won't say anything to the captain or the mate," Fargo generously offered.

"That's awful white of you." The roustabout grinned sheepishly and hastened around the corner.

The rest of the morning was less eventful. At noon the *Northern Lights* cast off from the dock and headed upriver, her great wheel churning. Maxton and his people pitched tents for the Stains. A table and chairs were set up in the shade and Pompey served mint juleps, of all things, to the ladies. Thomas and Charles and William Peel partook of Monongahela. Monique put out a bowl of pretzels for them to munch on.

It was a scene straight from a back lawn in New Orleans. One would never guess, to look at them, that they were in the heart of an untamed and largely unmapped territory.

Fargo was on a stump by the river, skimming flat stones, when William Peel came slinking over.

"My cousins would like you to join them."

"But you would rather I was on the *Northern Lights*." Fargo skimmed the last stone and it skipped seven times before it sank.

"I told you my feelings toward you aren't personal," Peel said.

"And buffalo fly." Fargo shouldered past him and over to the table. The Stains were relaxed and casual although they were still dressed as if they were at a formal ball. They stopped chatting and looked up.

"Tomorrow is the big day," Thomas Stain said. "If there are any last minute arrangements you want us to make, now is the time to mention them."

"I hope you brought other clothes," Fargo said.

Peel was moving around the table to his chair. "We're not idiots," he said sourly. "Or would you have us go around in the hide of a dead deer, like you do?"

Refusing to be baited, Fargo said, "Buckskins last ten times as long as that silk you're wearing. They don't shrink after a rain or fall apart at the seams if a man sweats a lot. Mud and dirt wash right off." He plucked at the fringe on his left sleeve. "And the whangs can be cut off and used in all kinds of ways."

"Be that as it may," Peel said, "it will be a cold day in Hades before you'll catch me wearing them."

"Do what you want. You'll make the Sioux happy. Buckskins blend into the brush better and are harder to spot."

"Is that how you've survived so long without getting an arrow up your ass?" Peel mocked him.

Thomas Stain pursed his lips. "Enough, William. Mr. Fargo has a point." He turned to Skye. "But you needn't worry. We all bought riding outfits guaranteed to hold up to the elements. And I had the presence of mind to buy them in green and brown."

"You were smart," Fargo praised him. For all his ignorance, Thomas Stain tried hard. "So tell me. When do I find out where the ghost town is?"

"You don't," Thomas said.

"Then how do you expect me to guide you there?" Fargo had been given a thousand dollars, in advance, and he aimed to give them their money's worth.

"What I propose," Thomas responded, "is to give you directions in increments. A little more each day until we're there."

"Are you pulling these directions out of thin air?"

"I have access to a map, Mr. Fargo. Not a precise map, to be certain, but it gives directions and rough distances and mentions a few landmarks."

"Do you trust whoever drew it?" was the logical question for Fargo to pose.

"I didn't know the man personally, if that's what you mean. The mapmaker has been dead for decades. But he had a lot at stake when he drew it, so it should be fairly accurate."

"Should be." To Fargo it sounded similar to those fake Spanish gold maps sold to gullible greenhorns in Denver, Santa Fe and elsewhere. He said as much.

This time it was Amanda who replied. "Oh, we assure you, it's nothing like that. We're not after gold nuggets or silver ore or any of that nonsense. Peelville existed. The ruins must still be there."

"Peelville?" Fargo said with a glance at their cousin.

"Yes," Thomas said. "It was named after William's great-uncle. William is the one who found the material that brought us here."

Fargo remembered Finn's comment about a million dollars. "What's in this ghost town that's worth risking your lives over?"

"That's for us to know," Thomas said. "If word were to leak out, every cutthroat in the territory would be after us."

Word already had, Fargo wanted to say, but he didn't.

"I have complete faith you can find it," Thomas Stain said. "The army officers I spoke to said you're the most dependable scout on the continent."

"Were they sober?" Fargo joked. A pungent odor assaulted his nose, and he turned. He had not heard Foy come up, which was troubling. "What do you want?"

"Nothing from you." Oscar Foy smiled broadly at the Stain party, his gaze lingering on each of the sisters. "I wanted to say that if any of you fine people need anything, anything at all, you only have to ask."

"That's kind of you," Charles said.

Elizabeth Stain, whom Fargo rarely heard say anything, stirred in her chair and asked in a voice as melodious as music, "I was wondering, Mr. Foy. In all that vast collection of merchandise, are there any bars of soap?"

"Why, yes, ma'am," Foy said cheerfully. "I have all the lye soap you ladies will ever need."

"I wasn't thinking of us."

Fargo almost laughed when Foy reddened and gave a little bow and left without saying another word.

"Honestly, Beth," Amanda said harshly, "was that absolutely necessary?"

"If I were to go on breathing, it was." Elizabeth caught Fargo's grin, and returned it. "I'm sorry if I've embarrassed you yet again, dear sister."

It was the first inkling Fargo had of what she was like, and of possible friction between the sisters.

"I'm used to it by now," Amanda said. But she did not sound used to it.

"The problem with you," Elizabeth said, "is that you care too much about what people think. You always have to be the proper lady."

Amanda's face clouded. "There's something wrong with that?"

"Any virtue carried to an extreme can become a vice," Elizabeth said. "Or in some cases, a crutch."

"What are you implying?" Amanda flatly demanded.

"There's no denying the truth. You would rather be ladylike than let down your petticoats and live a little."

"How dare you!"

Thomas held up a hand. "Enough! I won't have this petty squabbling. The two of you are always at each other's throats, and frankly, I'm tired of it." He jabbed a finger at Elizabeth. "How many times have I told you we do not air our dirty linen in front of outsiders? And you—" he pointed the finger at Amanda—"how many times must I tell you that you should set an example for your younger sisters?"

Amanda said she was sorry. Elizabeth picked up a pretzel and bit into it with a loud crunch.

Thomas focused on Fargo. "Now then. Is there anything else we need to go over? Anything I might have overlooked?"

"You have guns for everyone, I take it?" Fargo had not thought to ask before, and he should have.

"For the men. But naturally I didn't think the women would need them." Thomas made the idea sound ridiculous.

"Naturally?" Fargo said. "What do your sisters do if the Sioux jump us? Scratch their eyes out? Or if a grizzly decides we're its next meal? Your sisters should have rifles and revolvers, both."

"But they've never fired a gun," Thomas said. "They don't know the first thing about firearms."

Emma stopped sipping her mint julep to say, "How hard can it be to learn? I like the idea. I doubt I can stop a bear with my hatpin."

"I'll rely on the men to protect me," Amanda said.

"You would." From Elizabeth.

Charles leaned forward. "I saw revolvers and rifles in the trading post. Perhaps Mr. Fargo would be so kind as to select weapons for the three of you?"

"A great idea, brother," Elizabeth said. "We'll take turns. I'll go first." Rising before anyone could object, she moved toward the building, saying over her shoulder, "Are you coming or are you just going to stand there like a lump of clay?"

Fargo quickly caught up and matched her stride. "You're doing the right thing."

"The right thing was not to come along on this stupid quest of theirs," Elizabeth said angrily.

"Why did you, then?"

"Because they're my brothers and sisters. Because blood is thicker than water and all that damned silly nonsense Thomas likes to spout." Elizabeth slowed and some of the stiffness went out of her bearing. "Pay no attention to me. As you may have gathered, I have a habit of saying things I shouldn't. Which is why they like it better when I'm seen and not heard."

"I'm not them," Fargo said. "You can talk my ears off if you like."

A smile spread across her face. "That was kind of you. But then, I've noticed you're not the uncouth lout we half expected you to be. A lot goes on between those ears of yours."

"Don't tell anyone. It's supposed to be a secret."

Elizabeth laughed. "That settles it. You're definitely nicer than you let on. Which is more than I can say for some of the others my brother has dredged up."

"You don't like Maxton?" Fargo asked. The other Stains seemed to be on friendly terms with him.

"He's always been respectful toward me but when I'm around him my skin crawls," Elizabeth said. "There's something about him, something I can't quite put my finger on, that makes me wish he wasn't along."

By then they were at the trading post. Fargo opened the door for her. She stepped past him, then abruptly stopped.

Maxton was at the counter talking to Oscar Foy. They stopped, and Maxton turned and smiled. "Miss Stain. Or may I call you Elizabeth?"

"You may call me Miss Stain."

Foy wiped his greasy hands on his shirt. "What can I do for you, ma'am? I have all sorts of things for women. Combs, brushes, bonnets, bustles, you name it."

"Do you have guns for women, as well?" Elizabeth asked.

Maxton's forehead knit and he asked, "Whatever for? My men and I will protect you from harm."

"And who will protect me from you?" Elizabeth smiled as if it were a joke but her eyes were not laughing.

"Honestly, Miss Stain, whose idea was this?" Maxton glared at Fargo. "Your brother hired me for a purpose. I have a job to do and I will do it well. You can count on that."

Elizabeth stepped to the counter, well down from where Maxton stood. "I never count on anyone until they have shown me they deserve to be counted on." She fluffed her hair. "As for you, I'm aware of your, shall we say, shady business dealings? Gossip has it you have your finger in every illegal enterprise in New Orleans. Hardly a flattering character reference."

"Need I remind you that your brother has his finger in some of those same enterprises?" Maxton responded.

"In some respects I don't trust him entirely, either," Elizabeth said. "So it's not as if I'm singling you out."

Maxton regarded her coldly. "You're not the only one who has heard gossip. That sharp tongue of yours has gotten you into trouble before, hasn't it? But I thank you for making your feelings clear." He touched his hat and strode out.

Foy did not waste a second. "If it's guns you're after, ma'am, I have a lot to choose from."

It wasn't an exaggeration. Rifles, carbines and shotguns lined a rack on one wall, and a glass case was filled with revolvers of all makes and sizes, as well as a dozen derringers.

"My word. I never realized there were so many kinds."

Fargo was debating which would be best for her when Elizabeth's hand suddenly closed on his wrist and her nails dug into his skin. He glanced up and saw the same thing she did.

Framed in the south window were the swarthy head and shoulders of a Sioux warrior.

9

It was only a glimpse. The face was there and then it was gone. Elizabeth started to say something but Fargo gripped her elbow and shook his head. She looked puzzled but she did as he wanted.

Foy, bent over the gun case, hadn't noticed. "A lot of people like Colt or Smith and Wesson or Remington but there are dozens of manufacturers, ma'am. See this here? That's a Starr. And this one? It's an Allen and Wheelock. And that there? It's British. A Beaumont-Adams."

"Oh goodness." Elizabeth was still looking at the window. She tore her gaze from it and studied the case. "I'll let Mr. Fargo choose for me. I'd warrant he's much more knowledgeable about firearms than I am."

"I know a little," Fargo said. Since Elizabeth had never used a revolver before, he selected a Massachusetts Arms Company .31 caliber. Small and compact with a large trigger guard, it could stop a man, but it didn't have much kick and would be easy for her to handle.

Elizabeth handled it dubiously and experimented cocking the hammer and letting it down. "I feel positively primitive."

Fargo helped her pick a holster. She also needed a rifle but most of Foy's were the larger calibers needed for bringing down big game like buffalo. He settled on a .32 caliber Maynard.

When they emerged into the bright sunlight, her brothers and sisters and Peel were still under the tree, drinking and eating and laughing. Maxton and his men were over at the corral.

"I feel like a walking armory," Elizabeth remarked. The pistol was strapped around her slim waist and she was holding the rifle as if she were afraid it might bite her.

"You'll scare any hostiles half to death," Fargo quipped.

She slowed and lowered her voice. "Speaking of which, what about the one at the window? Why didn't you want me to tell Mr. Foy?"

"I suspect he already knows. I found sign out back that Indians paid him a visit right before the steamboat showed up."

"Should I tell the others?"

"Not yet." Fargo had a hunch he wanted to follow through on.

"Very well," Elizabeth said. "But if Indians jump us in our sleep tonight, I'm holding it against you."

Emma's turn was next. The moment they entered the trading post and were out of sight of her family, she brushed against him and huskily whispered, "I'm hoping you and I can get together again. How about tonight?"

"We'll see," Fargo said. He did not tell her he might have something more important to do.

"You sure know how to make a girl feel slighted," Emma complained. "Most men would fall over themselves if I so much as winked at them."

Foy was waiting at the gun case, smiling out of pure greed. "Here you go, Miss Stain. The best pistol collection this side of the Mississippi River. American made, foreign made, single-action, double-action, whatever you want, I aim to please."

"What was that about action?" Emma asked.

Fargo answered her. "A single-action revolver must be cocked before you can shoot it. With a double-action you just squeeze the trigger."

"Why aren't they all the same?"

"Why aren't all dresses the same?"

"That's a ridiculous comparison. Dresses are different because no two women are the same and we all have our favorite fashions and colors and whatnot." Emma tapped the case. "Guns are for killing. How many different ways do you need to do that?"

Foy chuckled. "Why, ma'am, I've never thought of it that way. Maybe I should sell pink and purple guns with lace on them."

"You're making fun of me," Emma said. "I just don't see the point."

"To answer your question," Fargo began, "different guns have different uses. You wouldn't use a derringer to kill a grizzly, and you can't play cards with a rifle shoved up your sleeve."

"I see. Some guns are better suited to certain needs, is that it? But what's all that business about calibers?"

Fargo tried to make it simple for her. "The bigger or higher the caliber, the more likely it will stop whatever you're shooting at."

"Which one do you recommend for me?"

Again Fargo went through the process of picking a revolver and a rifle. The whole time, he watched Foy without being obvious. The trader was relaxed and friendly, and never once glanced at the window or the back door. It strengthened Fargo's hunch.

Emma insisted on buying a .36 caliber Remington with pearl handles because it was "pretty." The Spencer that Fargo chose for her, however, was much too "ugly," and she would not use it unless she absolutely had to.

Amanda was supposed to go next but she sipped her drink and said, "Ladies do not wear guns. I'll rely on the men for protection."

"We can't watch over you every minute of every day," Fargo warned.

"Be that as it may," Amanda said, "I will not stoop to their level. I do not believe violence is ever appropriate."

Fargo had met people like her before. Those who went through life with blinders on. Who thought they were somehow above the common herd and could live by their own set of rules. They usually learned the hard way that life in the wild had only one rule: kill or be killed.

"Very well," Thomas Stain was saying. "If she doesn't want a gun, she can go without. I'll assign one of Maxton's men to keep an eye on her at all times. Is that a suitable compromise?"

"She's your sister," Fargo said. There was only so much he could say or do. "Right now I'd like to look over your supplies to see if there's anything you missed."

"I doubt that we did, but you're more than welcome to check," Thomas said. "Pompey will assist you."

Fargo didn't need any help but the manservant was already moving toward the neatly organized packs and piles. "I bet you wish you were back in New Orleans right about now."

"Not at all, sir," the black man said. "There all I do is answer doors and run errands and wait on Mr. Stain. This is quite thrilling."

"I knew a man once who thought searching for diamonds in the Rockies west of Denver was a grand adventure. He ran into some unfriendly Utes."

"I see, sir. I'd still rather be doing this than taking one of Mr. Stain's suits to the Chinese laundry."

"Can't blame you there," Fargo admitted. "There's only so much of civilization I can take before my skin starts to itch." A week of women, whiskey and cards was his usual ration. Any longer, and he was fit to climb walls. "How long have you been with the

Stains?" They reached the packs and he bent down and opened one to inspect the contents.

"My whole life, sir. My father served his father. My son will probably be a servant to his son unless all that talk about freeing blacks and the North going to war against the South comes true."

The prospect of a clash was in all the newspapers. "What will you do if it does?" Fargo asked.

"I haven't thought that far ahead, sir. All I've ever done is butler for Mr. Stain. It's all I know."

"The Sioux won't care if you're black or white. You're still invading their territory."

Pompey had fine, even teeth. "You never give up, do you, sir? Why are you so sure some of us will die?"

"Are you much of a tracker, Pompey?"

"No, sir, I can't say as I am. I've spent most of my life indoors."

"A good tracker can tell a lot from tracks. The kind of animal, how much it weighs, whether it's male or female, how fast it was moving when it made the tracks. A good tracker reads the lay of the land ahead and pretty much knows where an animal is heading."

"You're saying people are like tracks? That you can read them the same way, and you're certain we're headed for grief?"

"Let me put it this way," Fargo said. "If I were you, I would refuse to go."

"I can't do that, sir. My father never ran off. I won't either. Mr. Stain counts on me, and he treats me decent."

First the maid, now the manservant, Fargo reflected. He'd tried, and whatever happened now was on their own shoulders.

Checking the provisions took over half an hour. Fargo couldn't find anything they had forgotten but he found a lot they could do without. The women had brought enough clothes to change every day for two weeks and never wear the same garment twice. One pair of shoes was not enough; each had three or four.

The men were no better. Thomas and Charles had brought suits and white shirts and shoes suitable for high society but not for crossing the prairie in the hazy heat of summer.

Fargo figured they would squawk and they did. Thomas called Maxton over but Maxton surprised Fargo by saying they should leave it up to him and do whatever Fargo thought was best.

"But what do you expect us to do with all the things you want us to leave behind?" William Peel protested. "We can't just toss them in the river."

"Why don't we have Mr. Foy watch over them until we return?" Amanda proposed.

"Can we trust him?" Peel wondered.

Fargo left them to their argument and walked to the Missouri. No one showed the least interest in what he was doing. He strolled into the trees, waited to see if anyone followed him, and when he was sure it was safe, he crouched and circled around to the rear of the trading post.

Hunkering in dense cover, Fargo leaned the Henry against his leg and folded his arms across his knees. An Apache could squat like that for days. He wasn't Apache but he stayed there without moving a muscle for over an hour. Then two hours. He was about convinced he should come back at sunset when the back door opened and out stepped Oscar Foy.

The trader was grinning and whistling to himself. Without hesitation he walked into the woods and wound through the undergrowth to the north.

Staying well back, Fargo shadowed him. Foy was no city dweller to be taken lightly. Twice the trader stopped and looked behind him but each time Fargo went to ground and wasn't spotted.

Foy's route took him to a winding ravine and along

it to where it opened out onto the plain. Fargo stayed at the south end of the ravine until the trader had gone out the north end, then cat-footed forward until he heard low voices. Climbing with extreme care, he removed his hat and raised an eye to the rim.

Eight Sioux warriors, all young and all painted for war, sat on their warhorses waiting for a ninth to finish talking with Foy. The ninth warrior was the same one who had peered in the trading post window. Fargo had never met him but he had a notion who it was: Broken Horn, the young warrior out to make a name for himself.

Foy and Broken Horn were conversing in the universal language of the plains tribes, sign language, interspersed with a few comments in the Sioux tongue. Broken Horn was fluent in sign but Foy made repeated mistakes and had to reform his fingers to get his points across. It made eavesdropping easy.

Sign language did not use basic words like "a," "the," and "and." Fargo had to fill them in mentally.

"We want many guns," Broken Horn was signing. "You promised guns when we come."

"You help me, I help you," Foy signed. "Do as I ask and we both have what we want."

"I do not like to wait, Skunk Smell," Broken Horn signed. "Why not attack the whites from the fire-boat this day?"

"I want to know what they are after. It is important. For this you can have all the guns they have, plus I will give you five rifles and a box of ammunition for each rifle."

"That is good," Broken Horn signed. "But you must not speak with two tongues, Skunk Smell. If you do—" Broken Horn held his right hand close to his right shoulder with his fingers curled, then slashed down and to the left. It was sign language for kill.

"I have always talked straight tongue with you," Foy signed. "I talk straight tongue now."

"What about the white women?"

"They mean nothing to me," Foy signed. "The women are yours to do with as you want."

Broken Horn's hands were idle a few seconds. "You do not care if we kill your own kind?"

Aloud Foy said, "To hell with them and the airs they put on." In sign he said, "I watch out for me. No one else. All the whites in this land could die and I would not care."

"You have no heart, Skunk Smell," the young warrior signed.

"Do we have a deal?"

"We have a deal."

Foy held out his right hand. Broken Horn looked at it, then slowly held out his own and allowed the trader to pump it. Suddenly turning, Broken Horn vaulted astride his mount and reined it around. At a gesture from him, the entire war party galloped off to the northwest, raising a dust cloud in their wake.

Fargo followed Foy back to the cabin. The trader was happier than ever and had a jaunty snap to his stride. Swinging wide to the south, Fargo retraced his steps along the bank of the Missouri until he was once again by the tents in the shade of the giant oak. It was a bit before the Stains and their cousin noticed him.

"Yes?" Thomas said. "What is it?"

"I have a question for you," Fargo said. "Think about it before you answer." He paused. "If I were to refuse to guide you and rode off, what would you do?"

"I would be mad, for one thing, and keenly disappointed," Thomas said. "But with or without you, we're leaving for the ghost town in the morning. Why? Have you changed your mind?"

"No," Fargo said. "I just needed to know." His own decision was already made. He would see it through to the end, come what may.

10

They rode out an hour after dawn.

Fargo wanted to leave at first light but there were delays. The women took forever to get dressed. Then the Stains insisted on having breakfast served by Pompey and Monique. When they were done, and he thought all was ready, he discovered Maxton's men didn't have the pack animals ready as they were supposed to.

Oscar Foy was amused by their antics. As they headed out, he stood in the doorway of the trading post, smirking and waving.

Fargo was in the lead. After him came Thomas and Charles and their cousin, William Peel. The three sisters, trailed by the servants, were next. Maxton and his four toughs brought up the rear, leading the pack animals.

Once they reached the edge of the belt of vegetation bordering the river, open prairie stretched before them, a vast sea of grass sprinkled with occasional trees and broken by intermittent hills, bluffs and gullies. The morning was hot, thanks to the unblinking yellow eye high in the sky. Hardly a whisper of wind stirred the air.

Fargo did not see any sign of Broken Horn's band but that was to be expected. The Sioux would not make their presence known until they were ready, and that would not be until after they learned what the

Stain party was after. For the time being, at least, Fargo had one less worry.

At noon they halted in the open and rested as best they could in the blistering heat. Fargo heard Thomas direct Pompey to set up a tent, and went over. "The tent can wait until nightfall. We don't have the time."

"But we're sweating to death," William Peel objected. "I've never been so uncomfortable in all my life."

Fargo refused to give in. "Get used to it. This is how things will be unless we're lucky and it rains."

More hours of travel under the relentless sun brought them to a series of low hills by twilight. Fargo called a halt and camp was set up. Pompey erected two large tents for the Stains and a small tent for Monique and another for himself. Maxton's men spread out blankets on the ground near the fire.

Soon stars blossomed. Coyotes yipped at the quarter-moon. Somewhere in the far distance a cougar screeched, and once a bear grunted sharply from out of the mantle of night.

Fargo sat with his back propped against his saddle and the Henry across his legs. Many of the others jumped at every sound, but not him. He was used to them. Their absence would be more alarming; it would indicate they had unwanted visitors.

Suddenly perfume wreathed him. Monique was at his side holding a cup of steaming coffee. "With Monsieur Thomas Stain's compliments," she said, dipping in a curtsy. "He would like you to join him in front of his tent."

"When I'm ready." Fargo accepted the cup and blew on the coffee. "How are you holding up?"

Monique turned wide eyes toward the ring of darkness. "I do not like this place, *monsieur*. It scares me."

"It should," Fargo said.

"I have heard many stories. About the red men who take hair. About beasts that tear people to pieces and eat them." Monique shuddered. "I would rather be back in New Orleans. But the Stains are paying me three times what I normally earn to come along, so here I am."

Fargo took a sip. The coffee was delicious, and laced thick with sugar. "Did you make this yourself?"

"Pompey is the cook," Monique said. "He is a man of many talents, that one. His family must miss him terribly."

"He's married?"

"*Oui, monsieur.* With six young ones to sit on his knee and have him tuck them in at night. He invited me over once. His wife is very kind, very gracious."

"How about you? No husband tucked away somewhere?"

"Not yet, *non.* I am not ready. Perhaps in five or ten years. Until then I do as I please." Monique grinned. "Or who I please." She turned on a shapely heel and flitted toward the tents, saying over an equally shapely shoulder, "I will tell Monsieur Stain you will be along shortly."

Only after he had drained the last mouthful did Fargo follow her. The Stains were feasting on sumptuous fare, courtesy of Pompey, and washing it down with fine wine. Thomas set down his long-stemmed glass, and frowned. "At last. I was beginning to think you weren't coming. Have a seat and help yourself."

Fargo sank down and leaned the Henry against his knee. "What's on your mind?"

"Increments, remember?" Thomas reminded him. "Tomorrow we must head northeast until we strike a stream."

"Just one of the landmarks my great uncle mentions in his journal," William Peel commented.

"A journal?" This was the first Fargo had heard of one. "Any chance you would let me have a look at it?"

"Not a chance in hell," William answered with undisguised glee. "No one except Tom and I have that privilege."

"Not even your other cousins?" Fargo saw Charles and Amanda both frown and knew he had struck a raw nerve.

"It's in their best interests," William said. "They can't be made to talk if they don't know where we're going. *Exactly* where," he stressed.

Charles sat up. "That's not the reason and you damn well know it. You haven't confided in us because you don't trust us."

"I've never been one to put my faith in others, even those related by blood. Except Tom, of course. I've shown him almost every page."

"You had to in order to get his backing," Charles said stiffly. "Without our financial help, your dream couldn't come true."

"I've offered all of you shares, haven't I?" William snapped. "What more do you want?"

Thomas nipped the brewing argument with, "Now, now. That's enough, both of you. Suffice it to say, Charles, all of us will be amply rewarded for our effort and investment."

"So you keep saying," Charles responded. "But there had better be as much as he claims or there will be an accounting."

Fargo noticed that Maxton and his men were listening but trying not to let on that they were.

"Squabble, squabble, squabble," Amanda said. "That's all this family ever does. Usually I refuse to take part but in this instance I have to side with Charles. You're too secretive, William, and I don't like it."

The last thing Fargo wanted was to sit there and listen to their bickering. Fortunately, just then several of the horses whinnied and stamped their hooves, giv-

ing him an excuse to jump up and run over to the
string. One of Maxton's men was standing guard, a
scruffy character by the name of Ames.

"What spooked them?" Fargo asked.

"Something is out there," Ames said softly. "I
haven't heard anything but I'd swear it on a stack
of Bibles."

Judging by the way the horses were staring into the
night with their ears pricked, Fargo agreed. "I'll have
a look." He walked past the end of the string, then
darted into the dark. A dozen strides out he hunkered
to let his eyes adjust. It could be a predator nosing
about, and they could not afford to have their horses
spooked. The Stain party would not survive a week
without them.

Fargo made a wide circuit of the camp. He was
convinced whatever had been there was gone. But he
did not return to the tents. Instead, he flattened and
crawled close to Maxton and his men.

Maxton was gazing across the fire at the Stains and
Peel and saying, "—patient, boys. We have to be patient. The whole thing will fall into our laps. Wait
and see."

"Do you think it's true?" one asked.

"About Peel's great uncle?" Maxton shrugged.
"They think it's true, and that's good enough for me.
The Peels always have been the black sheep of the
family."

"But why here?" the same man inquired.

"Can you think of a better place?" Maxton rejoined. "It's as isolated as can be. No one would ever
think to come after him, even if they found out where
he went. Pretty damned clever, if you ask me."

"I'd have sailed for Europe and changed my name,"
said another.

"They would have found him there eventually,"
Maxton said, "and they weren't the forgiving kind.

My guess is that—" Maxton stopped, then whispered, "Shhh. Here comes the darky."

Pompey approached around the fire. "Pardon me, gentlemen, but Mr. Stain would like to speak to Mr. Maxton."

"So he sent you to fetch me instead of coming himself," Maxton said. "Be a good little darky and tell him I'll be right there."

Pompey didn't move. "I don't like that word, Mr. Maxton."

"Which word? Darky? Everyone calls blacks that. Or are you one of those who thinks he's as good as his betters?"

"My betters, sir?"

"Anyone with white skin. There's been a lot of talk in the newspapers about how we're all equal, and how your kind should have the same rights whites do, but that's stupid."

"How is that, sir?" Pompey's big fists were clenched.

"Giving blacks the same rights as whites would be like giving them to mules. Your kind isn't smart enough to get by on their own. Blacks need us to look after them."

"I had no idea you felt this way."

"I'm not the only one," Maxton said. "I'd as soon ship you all back to Africa where you belong but it isn't up to me."

"My family has been in America for four generations," Pompey said. "We wouldn't want to go back."

"What you want doesn't matter. Whites are your natural lords and masters, and you should do as we tell you." Maxton slowly rose and handed Pompey his empty cup. "Here. Make yourself useful."

For a moment Fargo thought Pompey would strike him. But the manservant had incredible self-control.

"If you don't mind my asking, sir, are you one of

those who likes to don sheets at night and take part in cross burnings?"

"What if I am? What is it to you?" Maxton demanded. "I've never tarred and feathered any darkies, if that's what you're getting at. I've always believed a good whipping is all it takes to keep you blacks in line."

One of his men nodded at Pompey. "How about if we take a rope to this darky's back just for fun? I'm a little out of practice."

"Stain wouldn't like it," Maxton said, "and so long as he's paying us, we keep him happy." To Pompey he said, "After you, darky."

"I would appreciate it if you don't call me that, Mr. Maxton, sir."

The man on the ground thrust a finger at him. "We'll call you whatever the hell we want and you'll like it or else."

Maxton put a hand on the man's shoulder. "Now, now, Trint. We're here to protect him, remember?" His fingers tightened and Trint squirmed in his grasp. "It won't hurt us to be civil." He smiled thinly at Pompey. "If you don't like to be called that, then we won't. Fair enough?"

Pompey nodded and stalked off.

The man Maxton had squeezed rubbed his sore shoulder. "I hate playin' these games. I'll be glad when we can kill them and be done with it."

"That makes two of us," Maxton assured him. "Which brings us back to being patient, and not giving ourselves away before the time is right."

Fargo had overheard enough. Sliding backward, he rose and circled to the east to enter the camp near where he had left it. "Nothing out there," he said to the anxious Ames.

Morning was a long time coming. Fargo lay on his back with his head propped in his hands and wondered how in the world he had let himself be drawn into such a mess. The expedition, as Charles had called it, was a keg of black powder with a short fuse that could be lit at any moment. Between Oscar Foy and Broken Horn and Maxton's men and William Peel, it would be a miracle if any of them made it out.

Daybreak found everyone astir. Pompey fixed breakfast and they were under way half an hour after sunrise, a slight improvement on the day before.

Fargo trotted on ahead to scout the lay of the land. The stream that was supposed to be there, wasn't. He covered mile after mile and had about given up on locating it when he came to the crest of a low rise, and there, below him, meandered a ribbon of water. Grazing on the other side was a small herd of buffalo, a rarity at that time of year. Usually the animals were farther to the south.

"A hunt is in order," Thomas Stain announced when Fargo returned and told him. "Fresh meat for supper."

"I'll shoot one for you," Fargo offered.

"Nonsense." Thomas yanked his rifle from its saddle scabbard. "I've always wanted to down one of the brutes. A friend of mine says it's excellent sport." He fed a cartridge into the chamber.

"I'm with you!" William Peel declared. "Anything to relieve the boredom." He shucked his own rifle.

Charles wasn't so sure. "Perhaps we should let Mr. Fargo do it. Buffalo are formidable creatures."

"Stay here with the women if you want," Thomas said with clear scorn.

"But what if something goes wrong?" Charles would not let it drop. "Why take an unnecessary risk?"

"Life is a risk," Thomas said. "You've always been too cautious for your own good." He and his cousin galloped away, laughing and whooping.

"Why do I put up with him?" Charles asked no one in particular, and applied his spurs.

With a heavy sigh, Fargo followed suit.

11

Fargo hoped the buffalo had moved on but they were still grazing contentedly, about two hundred of the great shaggy beasts strung along the other side of the stream. He caught up to Thomas and William and cautioned them, "Pick the one you want and don't go near it until it's down and dead."

"Look at them all!" William Peel exclaimed. "Let's shoot as many as we can. Whoever kills the most wins."

"You would make a game of senseless slaughter?" Charles said. "One is all we need."

Thomas rose in his stirrups. "See that big bull by the bank! He's got enough meat on him to feed an army." So saying, he jammed the stock of his rifle to his shoulder and flew down the rise at a gallop.

"Wait for us!" William cried.

Fargo cupped a hand to his mouth and shouted to Thomas not to get too close but if Thomas heard him, he gave no sign. The buffalo stopped grazing and looked up, and at William's next whoop, the entire herd broke into thunderous flight to the southeast.

Water sprayed from under the pounding hoofs of their mounts as the Stains and their cousin crossed the stream. Fargo was only ten yards behind them but it might as well have been a mile. Again he shouted a warning. Again Thomas Stain either did not hear him or chose to ignore him.

The bull they were after was at the rear of the fleeing herd. A massive animal, six feet high at the shoulders and pushing two thousand pounds, it could hold its own against anything on the continent. Despite its bulk it could run as fast as a horse, and with its huge head lowered and its tail held high, it was virtually unstoppable. Except by a bullet. Thomas Stain fired from a range of over a hundred yards and apparently missed. He fired again, and William Peel got off a shot.

A buffalo stumbled, but it wasn't the bull. A cow running behind it nearly fell but recovered and plunged on, a spreading scarlet trickle on her flank.

Fargo inwardly swore. He hated to see an animal needlessly suffer. Now Charles was firing along with the other two. None scored a hit. Another minute and the herd would be out of range, which suited Fargo just fine.

Then Thomas' rifle belched smoke and lead and the bull pitched to its knees. Almost instantly the shaggy behemoth was upright and running, but much more slowly, its head swinging from side to side with every bound.

A choking cloud of dust arose. The Stains and Peel galloped into the thick of it, and soon they and the bull and most of the herd were lost to view. "Rein up!" Fargo bawled, to no effect. A rifle cracked, and another. Someone shouted, the cry drowned by the din.

The dust was all around Fargo and the Ovaro. He slowed and heard another shot. Peel hollered something about the bull being down. "Don't go near it!" Fargo stressed, and drew rein. Only a fool blundered blindly about when a wounded buffalo was in the vicinity.

Bit by bit the dust began to settle. Vague shapes materialized. Fargo clucked to the stallion, glad to see the Easterners were still on their horses. They had ringed the bull and were admiring it.

"Look at the size of this monster!" Thomas crowed. "It could rip us apart without half trying."

"Let's shoot it again for good measure," William Peel suggested, and suiting action to words, fired into the bull's side.

Uttering a loud snort, the buffalo came up off the ground in a rush. It was on them before they could blink, its head down, its curved horns poised to rend. A burst of explosive movement brought it next to Charles, and before he could rein out of its way, the bull had slammed into his sorrel with the impact of a steam engine. Both Charles and his mount crashed down, the sorrel squealing in pain and terror.

Thomas snapped off a shot but his own horse had reared and he missed. William had the same problem with his.

Only Fargo had a clear shot. He brought up the Henry but the bull was quicker. It slammed into Charles as he rose to his knees. A horn caught him flush in the chest and sheared through his ribs like a sword through wax. The next instant the bull swung him overhead and tossed him like so much straw on a pitchfork.

Charles never cried out, never resorted to the revolver at his side. His arms and legs flapping, he hung as limp as a wet rag until the bull's next toss sent him sailing a dozen feet to land in a crumpled heap.

With that the bull was off, loping after the herd.

Thomas uttered a loud cry and spurred his horse after it, firing as fast as he could work his rifle, but the bull soon outdistanced him, and he reined around. By then Fargo had dismounted and carefully rolled Charles over. The horn had shattered the sternum and pierced through to the heart.

"Damn," William Peel said. "That was a stupid way to die."

"It could have been you." Fargo would rather it

had been; Charles had been the only reasonable one of the three.

"I'll die when I'm eighty and not before," William predicted. "I have too much living to do."

Thomas reined up and sprang down. Kneeling, he cradled his brother's head and bowed his own in sorrow. "This is my fault. I dragged him along even though he didn't want to come."

"If anyone is to blame, it's me," Peel surprised Fargo by stating. "The whole expedition was my idea from the start."

"My sisters will be heartbroken," Thomas said forlornly.

Fargo refrained from commenting. He had done his part. He had warned them and they had refused to listen, and their folly had cost a life.

"Want me to go tell them?" Peel asked.

Thomas shook his head. "It's mine to do. I just pray they can find it in their hearts to forgive me." He closed his eyes and for a long while was still.

Peel fidgeted in his saddle. He kept twisting from side to side and screening his eyes from the harsh glare of the sun with his hand. Finally Fargo asked him what he was doing. "Watching for savages, of course," was the curt reply. "They might have heard the shots."

"A little late to be thinking of that," Fargo said.

The sorrel was still alive. Its internal organs had oozed from the gaping wound but every so often it feebly kicked or lifted its head to nicker. It would linger in agony for hours unless something was done.

Rising, Fargo walked over. He pressed the Henry's muzzle to its head. The sorrel looked at him and he looked at it, and squeezed the trigger. At the blast its eyes rolled up and its tongue lolled out, and all signs of life ceased.

"Was that absolutely necessary?" William Peel asked.

The man would never know how close he came to being pulled down and beaten senseless. Wheeling, Fargo strode to the Ovaro and forked leather. "I'll bring a pack horse for the body."

"No need." Thomas gazed bleakly around him. "We'll bury my brother here. It's as good a spot as any."

The women and Maxton were half a mile away, taking their sweet time. Maxton rode ahead to meet Fargo and asked, "Where are the others?" But Fargo didn't answer. His expression forewarned the sisters, who fell grimly silent as he came to a stop and leaned on his saddle horn.

"Thomas or Charles?" Amanda asked.

Interesting, Fargo thought, that she was not concerned about Peel. Aloud he said, "Charles."

"How bad is it?" From Emma.

"Oh, God," Elizabeth blurted when Fargo shook his head.

The burial was a somber affair. Maxton had his men dig the grave. They grumbled and did so grudgingly, and when they were done, stood to one side, sullen, sweaty and dirty.

Elizabeth and Emma wept but not Amanda. She looked more mad than sad, and when Thomas stood at the head of the grave to say a few words in parting and quote from Scripture, she glared at him the whole time. It was plain she blamed him.

William Peel put on a show of being deeply sad but Fargo suspected it was a sham. Peel and Charles had never been all that close. It was Charles who had been the most outspoken against the Dakota venture, and had only tagged along because his brother and sisters were involved.

Fargo stood well back with Pompey and Monique. At one point the big black man commented softly, "He was a decent man, Charles Stain. He never once treated me with disrespect."

Monique was sniffling. "*Oui*. He was always nice to me, as well. He never yelled at me if I made a mistake, unlike his sisters."

"It's always the good ones who go first," Pompey observed. "The bad ones last longer because they're meaner." As he said it, he looked directly at William Peel.

"Maybe now we will give this madness up," Monique whispered. "Maybe now they will come to their senses."

"I wouldn't count on it," Pompey responded. "Thomas likes to finish what he starts. Now that he's lost his brother, he'll be more determined than ever to see this through to the end."

"We are stupid to be here," Monique said.

They pitched camp right there. Fargo left to rove in a wide loop in search of sign. He found none. If Broken Horn was out there, the young Sioux was shadowing them from a distance.

Half a mile to the south Fargo spied a shaggy brown hump. It was the buffalo bull, dead, with four bullet holes, two of which had bled so profusely there was hardly a drop of blood left in the giant body.

Fargo dismounted and cut off a haunch and took it with him. A lone buzzard was circling as he rode off. Soon other scavengers would show up. By morning there would be little left.

Pompey roasted thick steaks for supper. Maxton's men ate with relish but the Stains, understandably, did not have much of an appetite. Amanda picked at her food and then went into a tent. Elizabeth and Emma went for a walk along the stream.

Fargo ate by himself, on a log beside a pool. He was about done when a shadow fell across him and Thomas Stain sat down beside him.

"Mind some company?" Stain produced a pipe and a tobacco pouch and began to tamp tobacco into the bowl. "I owe you an apology, Mr. Fargo."

"How so?"

"I should have listened to you. Now my brother is gone and I'll bear the burden the rest of my days."

"It's not too late to save the others. We can pack up in the morning and head back before anyone else ends up the same way."

"I'm tempted," Thomas said. "But if we give up, Charles will have died in vain. I can't have that, I'm afraid. I'm committed, whether I want to be or not."

"And your sisters? Don't their lives mean anything?"

"That's an insult. My sisters mean more to me than anything. I just had a talk with them and tried to convince them to go back alone but they refuse."

"You could make them," Fargo suggested.

Thomas Stain laughed. "You don't know much about women, do you? Trying to force a female to do something she doesn't want to do is like trying to move a mountain. It can't be done."

"Then your brother did die in vain."

Thomas pulled the tie string to close the pouch and slid the pouch into a pocket. "You're implying I haven't learned my lesson? Quite the contrary. Or do you honestly think I want my sisters to come to harm?" He lit the tobacco and puffed a few times. "This affair is more complicated than you know. Our family's future depends on the outcome."

"You're supposed to be well-off," Fargo remarked.

"We were. My grandfather was quite the businessman. He left my father several hundred thousand dollars, and my father, in turn, divided it up among us when we came of age. But I've lost most of my money in bad investments. Elizabeth and Emma squandered their shares on frivolous nonsense. Amanda has a goodly sum left, and so did Charles, but the rest of us need to replenish our bank accounts or face financial ruin."

"And finding the ghost town will do that?"

Thomas ignored the question. "When one is desperate, one grasps at straws. Our cousin, William, is in the same predicament, only worse, thanks to his fondness for gambling. When he heard about my own difficulties, he came to me with his mad scheme to fill our coffers with more money than we had before."

Fargo bluntly asked, "Do you trust him?"

"He's my cousin," Thomas said. He then fiddled with the pipe and said softly, "He doesn't inspire much confidence, I'll admit. But he's related to us, and the Stains always stick by their own."

"What does Peel get out of all this?"

"Half of what we find," Thomas said. "Since I've had to bear most of the expense, the other half is mine, to divide up among the rest as I deem fit." He paused. "Charles didn't even ask for a share."

Fargo watched a small fish rise near the surface and swim back down. "It would help if I knew what you're after."

"We've tried to keep it a secret," Thomas said. "We were afraid that if word got out, we would be up to our necks in cutthroats of every stripe. Yet another reason I hired Mr. Maxton. As it is, even though William and my sisters have been sworn to silence, I can't be certain our secret is still safe."

"Meaning you won't tell me."

"At this stage it can't do any harm. But you won't believe me. Or you'll think I'm insane."

"Try me," Fargo said. At long last he would learn what it was all about.

Thomas lowered the pipe. "Very well. What is the last thing you would ever expect to find in the middle of Dakota Territory? No, don't answer. You would never get it right in a million years." He grinned. "We're after pirate treasure."

12

Skye Fargo gazed across the gurgling stream at the rolling grassland. Far to the southwest antelope were on the move. Much nearer, a prairie dog emerged from its burrow and stood on its hind legs to survey its domain. A small dust devil danced across the prairie, and the cottonwoods rustled in the breeze. "We're a long way from the ocean."

"I knew you would think I'm crazy," Thomas Stain said. "But there's a perfectly logical explanation."

"Next you'll be telling me pirates have given up attacking ships and are after wagons trains," Fargo joked.

"The pirate in question is Benedict Peel, William's great uncle, named after a famous general. Benedict was a scoundrel and a scalawag. At twelve years of age he was in trouble with the law for stabbing another boy in a quarrel over marbles. The boy lived and Benedict was let off, but at fourteen he killed his first man in a dispute over cards. He fled, and fell in with the wrong crowd. One thing led to another and he found himself a member of Jean Laffite's crew."

Fargo had heard of Laffite, a pirate, smuggler and slave trader famous for the part he played in helping to save New Orleans from the British many years ago.

"Laffite ran a large illicit empire," Thomas Stain was saying. "He operated out of Barataria for a while, but later, after the authorities threatened to run him out, he set up a new base on Snake Island. Galveston, it's called now. Eventually the government decided they'd had enough and sent a military force to destroy the pirate colony once and for all."

Again, Fargo was familiar with the account. Jean Laffite was a legend all along the Gulf Coast, and still talked about when men were in their cups.

"Laffite was too smart to go up against the United States Navy. He burned the town he had built, Campeche, and set sail for parts unknown. Some of his followers went with him. Others scattered to the four points of the compass."

"Among them Benedict Peel?"

"Exactly. Laffite had divided up a goodly portion of his treasure among his men, and Peel and five others wound up with a chest brimming with gold coins, ruby-encrusted goblets and more. They were to share and share alike but greed took over, and Benedict slit their throats while they slept and claimed the chest for himself." Thomas stuck the pipe stem in his mouth. "He was wealthy beyond his wildest dreams but he had a problem. He couldn't just walk into a bank and deposit the chest for safekeeping. As ill-gotten gains, it would be confiscated and he would be clapped into irons."

"He needed to hide," Fargo said.

"The authorities weren't his only worry. The pirates he murdered had friends, and he was afraid they would find out and come after him. But no matter where he went, in the States or in Europe, sooner or later they would find him. Benedict decided he needed to do as Laffite had done and set up his own colony. Only it had to be far from his old haunts, far from the sea and the men who flew the skull and crossbones."

"So he came here?" Fargo marveled.

"Why not? The frontier was largely unknown back then. Benedict thought he could start his own settlement and rule it as Laffite ruled Campeche. He would be safe from the law and safe from reprisals by other pirates." Thomas glanced at him. "It makes sense, doesn't it?"

Fargo had to concede that it did.

"Anyway, Benedict made the rounds of various dives and taverns and hired twenty scurvy river rats to do his bidding. He sealed the chest and brought it up the Missouri River on a keelboat, then struck off overland until he came to a spot he liked." Thomas blew a puff of smoke. "Peelville was born."

"A pirate on the prairie." Fargo chuckled to himself. Sometimes life was too strange for words.

"Benedict sent men back down the river for more provisions, and for women of loose morals. Pretty soon Peelville had half a dozen buildings, and work was being done on his mansion, which he patterned after Laffite's. Then a problem arose."

Fargo could guess. "Along came the Sioux."

"Apparently the Indians had been spying on the settlement for some time, wondering what the white men were up to. Soon after the women arrived, they struck. Eight river rats were killed before Peel's men drove the war party off. But their guns couldn't hold over a hundred Sioux at bay forever."

"They hightailed it out of there?"

"Benedict Peel had all the women climb into wagons and the men ride escort. They fled with just the clothes on their backs. He had to leave his cherished chest in his unfinished mansion. Exactly where, I don't know. William hasn't shown me that part of the journal yet and won't until we get there."

"Nice of him."

Thomas ignored the comment. "Benedict had gone to school as far as the sixth grade. He could read and write, and he scribbled a record of his day-to-day life. Everything from his favorite drink to his escapades with the ladies."

"How did your cousin get his hands on it?"

"I'm coming to that. You see, Benedict and his people hadn't gone five miles when the Sioux struck again. All but four of his men were killed and all the women were carried off. Benedict had an arrow in the back and another in his left leg but he had his men pull them out. They made it to the Missouri River where they hailed a boat and were brought down to New Orleans. His leg became infected and he became half delirious. He showed his brother the journal and tried to talk him into going after the treasure chest but his brother didn't want any part of it. Benedict died broke and bitter."

"No one has gone after the chest since?" Fargo inquired.

Thomas shook his head. "The brother's son found the journal in his effects after the brother died and gave it to his own son, William, who had little interest in it himself until his gambling debts piled up and he heard about my own financial setbacks. That's when he confided in me. And here we are." Thomas gestured. "I know what you're going to say."

"You do?"

"That this whole thing might be a wild-goose chase. That the Sioux or someone else might have found the chest already, and it's no longer there."

Fargo had been thinking something else. "Did anyone besides Benedict ever see the chest?"

"You're suggesting he made it up?" Thomas' brow knit. "Why would he do that? What other reason would he have for starting a settlement where no one had ever gone before?"

"The law was after him." For Fargo that was reason enough.

"But I've seen the journal. It has to be true." Thomas had a plaintive note to his voice. "It *has* to be." He slowly stood. "Wait and see. The chest will be there. We'll come back rich beyond our wildest dreams."

"There's one thing better than being rich," Fargo mentioned.

"Oh? What's that?"

"Being alive."

Thomas sighed and left him.

The sun was almost gone. Fargo stripped his saddle and bridle off the Ovaro and spread out his bedroll. No one had much to say. The Stains were still reeling from their loss. The three sisters turned in early but Thomas sat up late, sipping from a silver flask. At eleven he went into the tent he shared with his cousin and an argument erupted.

Fargo couldn't quite hear what they were saying. Not that it was any of his business. He pulled his hat brim low over his eyes and tried to doze off but sleep eluded him. Toward midnight he threw the blanket off. Only two people were still up. Trint was guarding the horses, and another of Maxton's men was playing solitaire. Neither noticed when he slipped out of the ring of firelight.

Moonlight cast the prairie in a pale glow. The coyotes were silent at the moment. Wings fluttered overhead but he could not tell whether it was an owl or some other bird. He cradled the Henry and began to circle the camp but a scuffing sound behind him caused him to whirl and level the rifle.

"It is only me, *monsieur*!" Monique whispered, throwing her hands in the air. "I saw you leave and followed you. I cannot sleep either."

"It's not safe out here," Fargo said.

"It is not safe anywhere, I think," Monique replied. "I am afraid all the time. I do not want to end like Charles."

"Put your arms down and go back." Fargo took it for granted she would do as he said and he turned to continue his check of the perimeter.

"I would rather not," Monique said. "Won't you let me walk with you, *s'il vous plaît*?"

Fargo was set to say no but the enticing allure of her short outfit and her bountiful cleavage gave him pause.

"I will be as quiet as the little mouse? I just need to stretch my legs, *oui*?" But it was her arms Monique stretched, swelling her bosom until her breasts threatened to explode from her maid's uniform. "I hope you do not mind?"

Fargo reminded himself that it was rare for the Sioux to attack at night. "Tag along if you want."

Grinning happily, Monique scooted to his side, her hand brushing his as they walked. "*Merci*. It is rare I enjoy a treat like this. To walk under the moon with a handsome man."

Fargo liked how her full lips were shaped. "I bet you've had your share of handsome gents," he flattered her.

"A few, perhaps," Monique said coyly. "But it is not something a girl should talk about, yes? Not if she is a lady."

"Texans have a saying," Fargo revealed. "There are two kinds of women in the world. Those who are ladies, and those who are still alive."

Monique chuckled, but not too loudly. "Which do you prefer, *monsieur*? A lady or a woman who is still alive? Is my virtue safe when you are around?"

"Only if you want it to be," Fargo answered.

"And if a woman did not want it to be, how could we go about it out here in the dark?"

The playful twinkle in her eyes was an invitation in itself. Fargo glanced toward the camp, then took her hand and led her to a dry wash a stone's throw away. Pebbles rattled from under them as they carefully descended an incline to the bottom. The sides were as high as Fargo's hat. "No one can see us here."

Monique gazed dubiously about, then flashed her dazzling smile. "I should have brought a blanket but it might raise eyebrows, *non*?"

"Why me, out of all the men? Not that I'm complaining, you understand."

"Who else is there? Amanda Stain would fire me if I so much as wink at her brother. Monsieur Maxton is too uncouth for my tastes, and those with him are pigs. Monsieur Peel would very much like to. He always touches me in places he should not touch when I serve him, and gives me looks. But he does not excite me as you do."

"Are you always this honest?"

"I would be lying if I said yes. I tell you the truth because I want you to like me, and so you will understand how much I like you."

Fargo set the Henry down, then placed his hands on her slender shoulders. She shivered as if she were cold and tilted her mouth up to meet his. He kissed her lightly at first but with increasing ardor as her soft lips parted and her silken tongue met his. Her small hands rose to his neck and she traced small circles with her fingernails. When they stepped back a minute later, they were both breathing heavily.

"*Mon Dieu!* You kiss nicely, *monsieur.*"

Fargo ran his right hand down her back and cupped her pert bottom. At the contact she stiffened and gasped.

"My, my. You are as hungry for me as I am for you, is that not so?" Monique reached behind him and cupped his backside. "What is good for the goose is good for the gander, *non*?"

"You jabber too much." Fargo smothered her hot lips with his and for a long while they were chest to breasts and thigh to thigh, savoring the taste and feel of each other's bodies.

Monique drew back and fluttered her fingers in front of her face. "You make me hot, *monsieur*. So very hot."

She was having an effect on Fargo, too. His manhood was as rigid as iron and straining for release.

"We're just getting started," he teased, and suddenly clamped his left hand to her mouth and whispered in her ear, "Quiet!"

Fargo had heard something. A faint sound that might or might not have come from near the wash. Stooping, he scooped up the Henry and crept to the rim. The prairie lay serene and undisturbed before him. He waited but nothing stirred and after a few minutes he went back down.

"What was it?" Monique breathlessly whispered.

"Nothing there," Fargo said, but he would have sworn he had heard something.

Monique clasped his hand and glanced nervously up and down the wash. "Maybe we should go back. There will be other nights."

"Whatever you want," Fargo assured her. When she didn't move, he bent and kissed her on the forehead and both cheeks and the tip of her nose. "Well?"

"I cannot make up my mind. You make my head swim, but I do not care to fall into the hands of the painted savages." Monique bit her lower lip. "What to do? What to do? I just don't know."

"Let me help you make up your mind," Fargo offered, and leaning the Henry against his leg, he enfolded her in his arms and bestowed the longest kiss yet, rimming her teeth and her gums and delving his tongue deep into her mouth. She responded in kind. Gripping her hips, he ground his pole against her, and she cooed like a dove. When he released her, her bosom was heaving and her skirt had hiked high on her thighs.

"That was not fair, my *joli* one." Monique was flushed with desire.

When it came to lovemaking and staying alive, Fargo did what he had to. "Do I gather that's a yes?"

"You tempt me against my better judgement. I have not had a man's hands on my body since the night before we left New Orleans, and I am not a nun."

"And I'm no monk. I like women as much as the next man."

"Is that so?" Monique's smile was masterfully seductive. "Prove it."

13

Their next kiss was molten. The night was cool but Fargo's blood was boiling when he lowered Monique to the grass and lay beside her. With her hair mussed and her maid's uniform askew and her lips parted in a delectable oval, she was a living portrait of wanton desire.

Fargo placed the Henry to one side but within easy reach. He undid his gun belt and set it next to the rifle, taking the precaution to loosen the Colt in its holster so he could grab it quickly if he needed it.

Monique arched her back and cooed, "What is taking so long, *chéri*? Must I take off my own clothes?"

In answer Fargo began undoing the tiny buttons at the base of her throat. Her uniform was patterned after the European fashion; undressing her was like unraveling a puzzle. But the prize was worth the effort, and presently the top half parted and her breasts jutted free. They were delightfully smooth and perfectly round with small nipples as hard as tacks. Fargo inhaled the right one and tweaked the nipple with his tongue. He felt her nails dig into his shoulder, felt her lavish wet kisses on his neck and ears.

Fargo cupped her other mound, and squeezed. Monique gasped and pressed her hips against his and her mouth fastened on an earlobe. She did things with her tongue that set his skin to prickling and his manhood to tingling.

Her perfume was intoxicating, a musky scent unlike any Fargo recalled. She had splashed some on her throat and her cleavage, and he inhaled it deep into his lungs as he lathered first one heaving breast and then the other.

"You are good," Monique whispered.

She had not seen anything yet, Fargo thought, as he bared her legs from the waist down. Her legs were shapely marvels, her thighs neither too heavy nor too thin but exquisitely right. He ran a hand down one and up the other, careful, for the moment, to avoid their junction. She was warm to the touch and squirmed in lustful anticipation.

"You make me wet."

Fargo would find out for himself soon enough. For now, he kissed her breasts and her neck, then fastened his mouth to hers and devoted both hands to fondling and pinching her breasts and caressing her hair. Bit by bit she grew hotter, ever hotter. Bit by bit her squirming became more heated, more urgent.

"Please," Monique pleaded.

Fargo was not quite ready. He sucked on her left earlobe while kneading her thighs, then parted her legs. She wrapped them around his waist but not too tightly just yet.

"I am burning up inside, *chéri*."

She wasn't the only one. Fargo resisted an urge to peel off his buckskins. He did not care to be caught with his britches down should the Sioux or something else come along.

The camp was quiet. A quick glance showed everyone had turned in except the sentry over by the horses. Fargo need not worry about discovery from that quarter. Bending, he licked from her throat, down between her breasts, to her navel. He swirled his tongue around and around. She gripped his hair in both hands and pulled, and his hat slid off and upended beside them.

"Why are you taking so long?" Monique complained.

Fargo placed a palm on each of her knees and rubbed upward in slow, small circles. Her inner thighs were wonderfully silken. He caressed one and then the other, until Monique was panting and tugging at his britches.

"If you don't do something soon, I will rip your pants off!"

Inwardly grinning, Fargo rose onto his knees and freed his manhood. Her mouth widened and she gingerly grasped him. Fargo thought he would explode. By a supreme act of will he was able to control himself, and aligned his member with her core. "Are you sure?" he teased.

"Damn you! *Oui*!"

Monique fed him in herself, inch by gradual inch, her eyelids fluttering, her chest rising and falling in great, gulped breaths. When he was all the way in she lay perfectly still with her eyes tight shut and her mouth oddly quirked.

"Are you all right?" Fargo asked.

"I have never been better," was her deep-throated reply, as Monique commenced moving her hips ever so slowly. She was drawing it out to make it last as long as she could.

Fargo didn't mind. Gradually the world around them faded. The grass, the stars, the night itself blurred into a darkling haze. There was her body and there was his, and that was all there was except for the pure pleasure that coursed through him in rhythmic ripples. He was adrift inside himself, and inside of her. He would thrust and she would rise to meet him, her head tilted back, her lips ripe cherries, her skin pale and sheer and velvet to the touch.

Fargo sucked on one nipple and then the other. He sucked on her lower lip and then her upper lip. He plunged his tongue deep into her mouth and she reciprocated. He massaged her bottom and the small of her back.

Monique whispered something in rapid French and rimmed her lips with the pink tip of her tongue. "Faster," she requested in English. "Harder."

All too willing to oblige, Fargo held on to her hips and rammed into her with ever more force and vigor. She shuddered at each thrust, her ankles locked behind him, her small body as taut as wire, her spine arched. Fargo lost all sense of time, of place. They moved as one for long minutes, until he began to wonder if she would ever go over the brink. Slipping a hand between them, he delved past her nether mount to the crown of her moist slit and her tiny swollen knob. One touch, one press of his finger, and she gasped and bit her lip and raised him clear off the ground.

"Oh! Oh! Oh!" Monique gushed and gushed.

Fargo held off a while yet. He stroked and stroked until his knees were nearly rubbed raw. Then his vision blurred, and he felt a familiar constriction in his throat. Fastening his fingers to her waist, he rammed into her as if seeking to cleave her in two. The explosion built and built and then Fargo was being pounded by dizzying waves of bliss.

Afterward, they lay in each other's arms. Fargo nearly dozed off but was he able to shake off the lethargy and sit up. Pulling himself together, he whispered, "We'd better get dressed and get back."

Monique slowly rose onto her knees and sluggishly rearranged her uniform. Several times she stifled yawns. A contented smile on her pretty face, she leaned toward him to breathe in his ear, "*Merci*. You were *très magnifique*."

Fargo helped her to her feet. Together they crept toward the ring of firelight. The sentry was leaning on his rifle, barely awake. No one noticed them. Fargo waited at his blankets until Monique was in her tent, then he sprawled out on his back and let himself drift into dreamland.

As usual, he was awake at the crack of dawn. He saddled the Ovaro and was ready to ride out before anyone else was up except Pompey, who had two pots of coffee on to boil and was making breakfast.

"Good morning, sir. What would you like to eat this morning?"

"A piece of toast will do."

"Is that all? A man should keep his strength up after a night like you had." Pompey smiled broadly.

"Me?" Fargo said in deliberate innocence.

"Monique went off by herself and was gone a long time," Pompey said. "It wasn't hard to add two plus two. She has too much self-respect to trifle with Maxton or any of his ruffians."

"Maybe she was stargazing."

"Don't worry, sir. My lips are sealed," Pompey promised, with a grin and wink.

Thomas and Amanda were up and ready but Elizabeth and Emma refused to come out of their tent. They wanted to spend the day in mourning for Charles.

Thomas refused. "The sooner we find what we came for, the sooner we're back in New Orleans. You have until noon."

Fargo poured himself a cup of coffee and sat beside Amanda, who looked as radiant as she had the first day he saw her. "You're not taking sides?"

"I try to stay out of their silly disputes as much as I can. It's pointless." Amanda sipped her coffee and watched Monique packing her things for her.

"Your sisters are quite upset about your brother," Fargo remarked.

"Implying I'm not?" Amanda arched a delicate eyebrow. "I'm as brokenhearted as they are. But I'm also mature enough not to let my emotions cloud my thinking. Tom is right. The longer we stay in this godforsaken territory, the higher the odds none of us will see home again. As you, yourself, have taken great pains to point out."

Thomas chose that moment to join them, muttering something about "females." To Fargo he said, "I've informed Mr. Maxton of the delay. Not that it matters to him. He's being paid the same whether our expedition take two weeks or two months."

"Surely not that long," Amanda said.

"We're not leaving Peelville until we've searched every square foot," Thomas said. "Belowground as well as above it."

Fargo remembered their talk about the pirate. "Doesn't the journal tell you right where to find the chest?"

Amanda jerked her coffee cup down, spilling some on her wrist, and glanced sharply at her brother. "You told him about the treasure?"

"Why not? He should know what's at stake." Thomas held out his cup and Pompey immediately filled it.

"Next you'll tell me Maxton knows," Amanda said tartly.

"I'm not stupid, dear sister," Thomas snapped. "He suspects, of course, that we're after something of great value, but he has no idea what."

Fargo said, "I wouldn't be so sure of that."

"Really?" Thomas gazed toward where Maxton and his men were readying the pack animals. "I'll have to keep a closer eye on him from now on. Although I'm paying him enough to temper his greed."

"How much is enough?" Fargo wondered.

"Seven thousand dollars. Five for him and two for his men. A fair amount, in my estimation."

Maxton undoubtedly disagreed, Fargo figured. Five thousand was nothing compared to the millions the chest must contain.

"Maxton notwithstanding, I couldn't take two months of this," Amanda said.

"If there's a way to do it faster, I'm open to suggestions," Thomas said.

"I can think of one," Fargo mentioned. "You and I can take the journal and go on ahead. If the treasure is there, we'll rig a travois and be back here in half the time it would take otherwise."

Thomas appeared to be considering the idea but Amanda gave a derisive snort. "Oh, sure. You would like that, wouldn't you? What's to keep you from helping yourself to the chest and leaving my brother dead in the dirt?"

"Sis!" Thomas said. "Don't insult the man."

"So what if I do? You're my brother and I love you dearly but you're too damned trusting. You let William talk you into this outrageous enterprise on no more proof than a musty old journal. You hired Maxton even though we hardly know him. Now you're willing to entrust your life to someone who might stab you in the back without a second thought." Amanda glanced at Fargo. "I'm sorry, but I won't be a hypocrite. Get mad if you want, but I don't trust you any more than I do Maxton."

"I don't blame you," Fargo said. In her shoes, he would feel the same.

Thomas, however, wasn't appeased. "Give me some credit, will you? I'm not a simpleton. I'm not going to accept Mr. Fargo's suggestion. I refuse to leave you girls here alone."

"We should never have come," Amanda said. "This isn't a grand adventure. It's lunacy."

"What's done is done," Thomas declared. "We have to see it through, for Charles' sake."

Amanda stared at him unblinking, then bowed her head and said softly, "We'll stick it out, then. But if you come to your senses and change your mind, I won't regret turning back. I like being alive, Tom."

"And I don't? Now you're being ridiculous." Thomas stood. "Just wait. You'll thank me when this is over."

Amanda did not say anything until he had gone into a tent. "Did you hear him?" She was asking herself, not Fargo. "Why is it men are so blind to what goes on around them?"

"He's doing what he thinks is best," Fargo said.

Amanda cocked her head and regarded him intently. "Perhaps, but it doesn't excuse the mistakes he's made. Mistakes that could cost me my life."

"Then why don't you head back?"

"Family comes before all else."

"Charles said the same thing." Fargo felt sorry for her. She was trapped by her love for her siblings, just as her dead older brother had been.

Hours passed. It was well past ten when Elizabeth and Emma emerged. Emma's eyes were misty and red and she couldn't stop sniffling. Neither was hungry but Pompey persuaded them to have some tea.

By noon they were on the go. Fargo trotted on ahead to scout the terrain. From the crest of a ridge he studied the broken country ahead, memorizing landmarks. About to rein around, he spied riders a mile to the west moving in single file, paralleling the Stains. He could not tell much about them but he knew who it was: Broken Horn and the Sioux war party.

An idea came to him. That evening Fargo took Thomas aside. "I'll be gone for a while," he said, and explained why.

Stain tried to talk him out of it, and when that failed, commented, "You're mad to go alone. Take Maxton and a couple of men along."

"They've never fought Indians. I have. It's better if I do this alone."

Thomas held out his hand. "In that case, be careful. Here's hoping you don't lose your hair."

It was a sentiment with which Fargo heartily agreed.

14

Broken Horn had camped in a hollow so the Sioux campfire could not be seen from a distance. The horses were bunched at the north end but had not been hobbled or tied. The warriors were hunkered around the fire, talking and joking, unaware they were being spied on from the rim.

Fargo had left the Ovaro in a draw, and after removing his spurs and placing them in his saddlebags, he had dropped onto his belly and crawled the last hundred yards. His plan was to run the horses off and leave the Sioux afoot. Without mounts it would take them weeks to reach their village and acquire fresh animals, and by then the Stains, with any luck, would be on their way back to civilization.

Broken Horn was talking. Fargo could not catch everything the young Sioux said but gathered it had something to do with a raid on an army wood detail. Broken Horn had counted first coup on several of the soldiers, killing one with an arrow through the heart.

All the warriors in his band were as young as he was. As young, and as eager to prove themselves. They stayed up late, until well past midnight; as each man wearied, he curled up where he was, and fell asleep. Because they were young, they were careless. They did not think to post a sentry.

Fargo waited another half hour to be sure. Then he backed away until he could not be seen from below, rose in a crouch, and stalked toward the north end of the hollow.

The wind was in his favor. It blew his scent away from the horses. When he was again near the rim, he flattened and snaked to the edge. Most of the warhorses were dozing. Only one had its ears pricked and was looking at him. He studied the slope and saw a gap in the west side.

Again Fargo crawled backward. Rising, he hurried to the Ovaro, stepped into the stirrups, and shoved the Henry in the scabbard. Undoing his coiled rope, he rode at a slow walk back to the hollow, and the gap he had found.

Drawing rein, Fargo verified the Sioux were still asleep. He hunched low over his saddle and moved into the hollow. None of the sleeping warriors stirred.

By now most of the horses were awake and watching him. His scent, so strange to them, provoked several into snorting. He angled around until he was behind them, careful not to get too close, one eye always on the Sioux. A husky warrior rolled onto his back and another mumbled in his sleep but none woke up.

Fargo had only a few yards to go and he would be where he wanted to be. Suddenly a paint whinnied and shied and stamped. In a twinkling several warriors were on their feet. The fire had nearly died out and it was several seconds before they realized something was amiss, long enough for Fargo to straighten and whoop like a Comanche while swinging his coiled rope overhead.

The Sioux horses did what Fargo wanted; they bolted toward the west side of the hollow and the gap that would take them out onto the prairie. But only one animal could make it through at a time, and when several tried, they ended up shoulder to shoulder, and hemmed by the horses behind.

Broken Horn yelled and warriors bounded to stop

them. A bow string twanged and a shaft buzzed inches from Fargo's head. Palming the Colt, he banged off a shot that pitched the bowman into the grass.

The horses were milling and nickering in rising panic. Several separated from the rest and started up the incline. Their hooves flailing, they dislodged a torrent of rocks and dirt and dust.

Another arrow sought Fargo. A lance fell a few yards short. He thumbed back the hammer and squeezed the trigger and a Sioux clutched at a shoulder and fell. His shots had the added effect of scaring the horses even more, and two reached the top and disappeared into the night.

Broken Horn was beside himself, screeching like a madman.

A plunging bay made it through the gap. Then another. Within moments the rest were galloping from the hollow with Fargo close after them. He made it out, arrows falling all around him.

Then the wind was in his face and Fargo shouted and drove the horses ahead of him. He had lost two or three but the rest were bunched together. He went over a mile before he drew rein and sat listening to the drumming of their hooves dwindle into silence.

"We did it, big fella," Fargo said, and patted the Ovaro. Attaching his rope to the saddle, he made for camp, riding at a leisurely pace. He arrived with only a couple of hours left until sunrise.

Fargo was tired but he did not feel like sleeping. Rekindling the fire, he made a fresh pot of coffee. He was halfway done with his first cup when Maxton came over and helped himself, a blanket about his shoulders.

"Mr. Stain told me what you were up to. How did it go?"

Briefly, Fargo related his success.

"I hope you're right and we've seen the last of them," Maxton said. "I can do without tangling with a bunch of red heathens. And before you say anything, it's not because I'm afraid of them. It's common sense. Why lose your hair if you don't have to? I'm sure as hell not losing mine for the Stains or William Peel."

"You're being paid a lot to protect them," Fargo said.

"Not nearly enough. I place a high value on my skin. Don't get me wrong. I'll do what I can, but I'm not taking a bullet or an arrow for anyone, not even the ladies."

"Do they know that?"

"I've never come right out and told them. Not that it will make a difference if the Sioux catch us off guard." Maxton squatted and held his free hand near the flames to warm it. "Mind if I ask you a question?"

"Depends," Fargo said.

"Nothing personal. It's about the Stains. About what you will do if you have to make a choice between saving them and saving your own hide."

"It might not come to that."

"But if it does," Maxton persisted. "Are you willing to throw your life away for three rich biddies who couldn't care less about you?"

"They're women."

Maxton chuckled. "I never have understood that way of thinking. So women wear dresses and we don't? That makes them special? Worth dying for? Hell, the only person worth my life is me."

"Do your men feel the same?"

"They do as I tell them." Maxton swirled the coffee in his cup. "It's you I need to know about. If things get rough, can I count on you to back me or the Stains? Where do your loyalties lie?"

Fargo was insulted. "Do you really need to ask?"

"No. I guess not. It's too bad, though. Nothing is as it seems. Hasn't been from the start. You've been played for a fool, and not by me."

"Save your lies for your men. You'd shoot me in

the back if you thought you could get away with it."
A chance Fargo was not going to give him.

Maxton rose and faced him. "You make it real easy
for me to do what I have to. Very well. It's on your
shoulders." He paused. "Thomas Stain has run things
long enough. Now that you've taken care of the Sioux,
it's time for a change. As of this minute I'm taking
over."

"Just like that?"

"No. First I have to dispose of you and the darky.
Then I'll roust out the others and make Peel hand
over that journal he thinks I don't know about. Then
it's on to Peelville. Your help is no longer needed."
Maxton raised his cup in a mock salute. "Save me a
spot in hell."

Too late, Fargo realized Maxton had been talking
to keep him distracted. Too late, he went for his Colt,
and whirled. He glimpsed Trint behind him, and a rifle
stock filled his vision. Pain exploded, and then there
was nothing, nothing at all.

His first sensation was of pain. Searing pain that
pounded his skull like the beat of a thunderous drum.
The next sensation was clamminess on the right side
of his head and half his face. He opened his eyes, or
tried to, and felt a surge of panic when the blackness
persisted. Was he blind? he frantically wondered.

Fargo realized his eyes wouldn't open because
something was keeping them shut. He tried again. It
felt as if they were glued fast. He tested his left arm
and gingerly groped about his face and hair. Both
were plastered thick with what had to be dried blood.
He pried at his right eyelid, careful not to cut or
scrape it with his fingernail, and a sliver of light grew
into full, dazzling vision.

It took a few moments to pry the dried blood off
the other eye. Blinking in the bright glare of the afternoon sun, Fargo grit his teeth against the pain and

slowly raised his head to look around. He was flat on his back in the same spot where he had been sitting when Trint tried to smash his head in.

Fargo started to sit up but a wave of dizziness brought on a general weakness in his limbs and he sank back down to catch his breath. He was frankly surprised to be alive. Maxton had wanted him dead. Maybe they mistakenly thought he was, what with all the blood, or else they believed he was so severely hurt he wouldn't last long on his own.

A groan brought Fargo up on his elbows. Someone else was nearby. He glanced right and then left and saw a tall dark form prone in the grass. "Pompey?" he croaked. His mouth and throat were so dry, he had to swallow several times before he could clearly say the manservant's name.

There was no response. Grunting against a new wave of torment, Fargo eased onto his side and pushed to his knees. Once more the world spun and he thought he would fall on his face but the vertigo faded. On hands and knees he crabbed to the big black's side. One look was enough to tell him it was hopeless.

Pompey had eight bullet holes in his chest, and blood was oozing from the corners of his mouth. Fargo placed a hand on Pompey's arm and the manservant's eyes opened and rolled wildly about before focusing on him.

"Mr. Fargo, sir, you don't look so good."

"Who did this to you?" Fargo asked. As if he couldn't guess.

"Maxton and his men. I saw Trint hit you and came to help but they pulled their pistols and shot me down." Pompey coughed and the blood oozing from his mouth became thicker. "Then Maxton came over and put three more bullets into me, saying as how he never did like darkies."

"The Stains and Peel?" Fargo asked.

"I don't know. I heard more shooting, and a scream."

Fargo raised his head, and an icy chill ran down his spine. Ten yards away lay someone else, facedown. Someone clad in a pretty dress. "It's one of the sisters. I'll be right back."

"I'll be here," Pompey said, mustering a grin.

It took every ounce of will Fargo possessed to rise to his feet. His legs nearly gave out and his stomach churned, but he stumbled woodenly to the body. He recognized the hair. "Emma?" he said softly. Sinking down, he gently rolled her over. She had been shot just once, smack between the eyes. They were wide with shock, and glazed. Turning his head away, Fargo closed her eyes, and swore.

"Mr. Fargo?" Pompey's voice was weak.

Rousing himself, Fargo went back. It would not be long. Pompey was breathing raggedly and the whole front of his shirt was stained scarlet. "I can fetch water from the stream."

"Don't bother. I'm not long for this world." Pompey's eyes shifted. "Who is that over there?"

"Emma Stain."

"They murdered her too? Why? What purpose did it serve?" Pompey let out a sigh. "She was such a nice girl, too." His fingers slowly rose to Fargo's arm. "Don't let them get away with this."

"If it's the last thing I do, I'll buck them out in gore."

Pompey began to nod, then stiffened. Clenching his teeth, he puffed noisily through his nose. "Never thought it would be like this. Figured to die of old age in bed beside my wife." Lines of deep sorrow marked his features. "My wife. My children. I'll never see them again. They'll never know how it was."

"I'll get word to them," Fargo offered.

"New Orleans. Fremont Street. Her name is Ernestine. Our last name is Clovis. Tell her—" Pompey stopped, his mouth partly open, his gazed fixed on the clouds.

"Tell her what?" Fargo prodded, and when no answer was forthcoming, he pressed a hand to Pompey's neck, feeling for a pulse. "Damn," he said, and for the second time in minutes closed a dead person's eyes.

Of the rest there was no sign. The tents, the horses, everything and everyone had gone off to the north, their trail as plain as a road.

Fargo wanted to bury Pompey and Emma but without a shovel it would take hours he couldn't spare. The best he could do was cover them with brush and rocks. That in itself exhausted him. His head pounded worse than ever and his stomach threatened to disgorge its contents.

Shuffling to the stream, Fargo eased onto his belly and dipped his head in the refreshingly cool water. It felt so good he did it several times, holding his breath as long as he could. Using a palm, he rubbed the blood off. He had a deep gash where the stock had struck him.

Reclaiming his hat, Fargo bent his boots northward. The burning sun, the pain, the dizziness, conspired to turn the trek into an agonizing ordeal. He discovered his holster was empty. They had taken the Colt as well as the Ovaro, but they had overlooked the Arkansas Toothpick in his ankle sheath. So he wasn't completely defenseless, although in the state he was in, he might as well be.

In a quarter of a mile he saw something in the grass. A travel bag. Someone had upended it, strewing female garments about. A little farther on there lay another. A long line of discarded items stretched for as far as the eye could see. Maxton had gotten rid of everything he deemed unnecessary, including all the clothes the women brought.

Fargo estimated they had a good six-hour start on him, if not more. Catching up would take some doing.

120

Thankfully, they were following the stream, so thirst wasn't a problem. His splitting head was another matter. Every half an hour or so he would stop and dip his head in the water.

Sunset found Fargo still plodding along. He craved rest, craved a solid ten hours sleep, but Maxton was bound to stop for the night. By morning, if he kept going, he could overtake them.

Gradually, the heavens transformed into an inky mantle sprinkled by a myriad of stars. The moon was conspicuous by its absence.

Fargo could have used the extra light. He was alone and virtually defenseless in a country teeming with savage men and beasts. His fatigue grew worse. He walked mechanically, his chin on his chest, his head always throbbing, throbbing, throbbing. Midnight came and went. He raised an arm to adjust his hat and spotted a telltale pinpoint of reddish-orange light off across the prairie. He had done it! Another couple of hours, and Maxton was in for a shock.

Then the undergrowth to his left crackled with the passage of a large animal, and a guttural growl sent Fargo hurrying to the nearest tree. Wrapping his arms and legs around the trunk, he shimmied up and hooked a leg over a limb. Below him the undergrowth parted and out strode a bear. In the dark he mistook it for a black bear until it came to the base of the cottonwood and reared onto its hind legs. That close, he could see a distinct hump.

A grizzly wanted him for its supper.

15

Skye Fargo clung to the branch as the bear braced its huge forepaws and a menacing growl rumbled from its massive chest. Its maw gaped wide and fangs gleamed in the starlight.

The bear sniffed a few times, then threw all his weight against the tree, shaking it violently. Even though he was holding tight to the branch, Fargo was nearly dislodged. By throwing an arm around the bole and wedging a knee in the fork, he retained his perch.

Undeterred, the grizzly shook the tree again and again. When that didn't work, it stretched as high as its height allowed but its claws were inches short of the branch.

Instinct compelled Fargo to scramble higher. Just as he did, the bear threw itself upward. Its gnashing teeth narrowly missed his right boot. Then the grizzly fell back, thwarted, and vented its anger with tremendous roars that seemed to shake the very ground.

Fargo recollected tales he had heard of frontiersmen treed for days by hungry bruins. A Cheyenne of his acquaintance once spent over a week high in an oak after a pair of grizzlies took turns waiting at the bottom for him to descend. Only the fact he had a parfleche filled with pemmican saved the Cheyenne's life. He outlasted the devils; they lost interest and drifted off.

Fargo did not have a parfleche. He did not have

any food at all. The stream was twenty yards to his west but he wouldn't live to reach it as long as the bear was there.

The grizzly redoubled its assault. The cottonwood shook and swayed but it was too thick for the grizzly to break or bend and too thin for it to climb. In pure bestial rage it tore at the bark, ripping off large chunks. Then it stopped and dropped onto all fours and prowled in a circle, its eyes fixed on Fargo the whole while. He made a few choice comments on the bear's lineage that provoked another roar. After that there was nothing for him to do but sit and wait and hope the grizzly became hungry enough to go after easier prey.

From his new vantage point Fargo saw the distant campfire more clearly. A few figures were sprawled near it, apparently asleep.

Unexpectedly, the grizzly moved toward the stream. Fargo's hopes rose but the bear was only slaking its thirst. In a few minutes it was back, tirelessly walking around and around the trunk.

Fargo made himself as comfortable as he could. Unfastening his gun belt, he looped it around a branch and slid his left arm through the loop. Then, using the same arm as a pillow, he closed his eyes and tried to doze off. The hammering in his head wouldn't let him.

Disgusted at the turn of events, Fargo sat back and strapped his gun belt back on. The bear was still down there, growling whenever he moved. "What I wouldn't give for my Henry."

The night dragged by. Dawn broke crisp and clear. Fargo shifted to relieve a cramp and the grizzly growled and came over to the cottonwood and swiped at it several times, leaving long furrows.

Well to the north, stick figures broke camp and shortly thereafter stick riders filed out of sight.

Fargo glared at the bear. He had been so close. Now he must go through the hell of chasing them on foot all over again. Furious, he broke off a small branch and threw it at the grizzly. His aim was good. It struck the brute on the head but the bear didn't even blink.

Birds were warbling along the stream. A butterfly flitted from flower to flower. On the opposite bank a doe and two fawns timidly neared the water's edge to drink, caught wind of the grizzly, and fled.

Suddenly a faint shout fell on Fargo's ears. He twisted to the north and leaned as far out as he dared. A rider appeared, riding like a madman. Or madwoman, since Fargo saw that the rider wore a dress and had straw-colored hair and was lashing her mount in a frenzy of fear. With good reason.

Maxton and Trint were in pursuit. Trint banged off two shots from a rifle. Apparently Trint was not trying to hit her. Both shots missed. They were playing with her, and they cackled when she cried out.

The grizzly had risen onto its rear legs and was watching the spectacle with interest. Whether it would run or attack was impossible to say. As Fargo had learned the hard way, bears were the most unpredictable creatures on God's green earth.

Elizabeth was sobbing. She knew she could not escape. Her flight would take her hundreds of yards east of the tree Fargo was in. He pumped his arm to signal to her to ride in his direction but just then Trint fired a third time and the mare Elizabeth was riding squealed and went down in a tumble of legs, tail and mane. Elizabeth was thrown clear but she was dazed and slow to gain her feet.

Maxton and Trint separated to come at her from different directions. Maxton shouted something and laughed, and Elizabeth put a hand to her mouth, turned, and ran. She had taken only a few steps when Maxton's rifle barked.

Elizabeth flung out her arms as she fell. He had shot her in the left leg. She propped her hands under her and was rising when he fired again and a slug cored her other leg. She had to be in great pain and she was bleeding profusely but she crawled toward a willow, dragging her legs behind her.

Maxton and Trint drew rein, and Maxton slid from his saddle. Smirking sadistically, he ambled toward Elizabeth. She crawled faster but he slammed her down with the heel of his boot. He said something, and kicked her in the ribs. Doubling up, she answered him.

They were too far away for Fargo to hear them. He started to climb down and was reminded why he shouldn't by a threatening growl.

If only he had a weapon, Fargo thought. Then it hit him. He did. If he could lure Maxton and Trint in close, the bear might take care of them for him. But as he went to yell, Maxton shot Elizabeth Stain in the back.

Red-hot rage coursed through Fargo. He saw Maxton nudge her, then turn and swing onto his mount. The killers headed back the way they had come, leaving a still form in the dust.

The grizzly dropped onto all fours and moved toward them. Fargo hoped it would give chase. Over short distances a griz could outrun a horse. But it wasn't interested in Maxton and Trint. It was making for Elizabeth.

Lowering himself from branch to branch, Fargo slid the last twenty feet, nearly scraping his palms raw. He drew the Arkansas Toothpick and sprinted after the bear, intending to stop it but unsure exactly how. Her horse solved the problem for him. The mare was still alive, and vainly striving to stand.

The grizzly slunk forward as stealthily as a cougar. When it was thirty feet from its stricken quarry, it roared and charged. The mare twisted her head and desperately tried to stand. Her head and neck were an inviting target. The bear's iron jaws closed like twin vises, and a crimson geyser spurted. Drenched red by the deluge, the grizzly dragged the mare into the woods.

Fargo bent low as he emerged from cover. "Elizabeth?" he whispered, leaning over her. She had a pulse but it was pathetically weak. Cradling her in his arms, he carried her in the direction opposite of where the grizzly had gone. In a small clearing sheltered by pines he set her down. "Elizabeth? Can you hear me?"

"Fargo? You're alive?"

He had to place his ear near her lips to catch what she said. Gripping her hand, he whispered, "I'm sorry. There was nothing I could do."

"Not your fault." Elizabeth's eyes mirrored a calmness Fargo did not share. "I thought I could get away. I was wrong."

"The others?"

"Maxton shot Tom in the shoulder but Tom is holding on. His men roughed up Amanda and did terrible things to Monique." Elizabeth's voice was growing weaker with every word she spoke.

"And Peel? Has he told Maxton where to find the treasure chest?"

"He doesn't have to. Maxton has the journal. But he's keeping William alive for now." Elizabeth swallowed. "There's hardly any pain. Why should that be?"

"Sometimes there isn't," was all Fargo could think of to say.

"Do me a favor. Kill them. Kill the sons of bitches dead as dead can be. And mention my name when you do."

"You shouldn't talk," Fargo said.

"I should lie here and die quietly? There will be enough quiet on the other side of the grave." Elizabeth slid her hand toward him and he clasped it. "Emma told me about the two of you. She said you're the best lover she ever had. Too bad. I would have liked to find out for myself."

"Can I get you some water?"

"What I would like is a kiss," Elizabeth said. "Please. Before it's too late. Just one little kiss."

"Whatever you want." Fargo lightly pressed his lips to hers, and as he did, she went limp. She breathed her last breath into his mouth. Scowling, he picked her up and carried her north. He would be damned if he would leave her for the grizzly to find. He walked until he came to the charred embers of their campfire. Past it was a gully. He covered her with loose stones and whatever else was available, and moved on.

A second day on foot under the hot sun did not appeal to him but he couldn't lie up until evening. He would lose too much ground. On he hiked, mile after tiring mile. By evening he yearned to rest but he refused to stop. Maxton would soon make camp.

Night fell. Fargo was crossing a broad plain when without warning gunfire crackled, coming from hills to the northeast. Rifles and pistols in a leaden chorus punctuated by strident whoops and yips. He did not know what to make of it until the tracks he was following bore toward the same hills.

The din had long since quieted. He covered half a mile in unnatural silence. Then hoofs sounded, and three or four riders passed him to the west. He had to guess how many; he couldn't see them.

Darkness shrouded the hills. Fargo advanced warily, and abruptly spied what appeared to be a man with his back to a boulder on an adjacent slope. Thinking it was a sentry he crouched down, but when no one challenged him and no shots thundered, he ventured closer.

One of Maxton's men had gone down fighting. He had three holes in his chest, but not bullet holes. These had been made by arrows, which had been pulled out. It was customary after a fight for the Sioux and other tribes to retrieve their shafts if they could to spare themselves from having to make more.

The man's revolver was gone. So was a knife that had been in a leather sheath on his left hip. Fargo checked for a hideout under the man's shirt but there was none. He was about to turn away when he thought of his own ankle sheath. The man's right boot was empty but in the left Fargo found a two-shot derringer. Both barrels were loaded. It wasn't much but it was better than nothing, and he slid it into a pocket.

Two questions had to be answered. First, where were the others? Second, who riddled the gunman? Had Broken Horn's war party caught some of their horses or were other Sioux in the area?

Fargo started up the hill. From the top he would be able to see for miles. He had passed several boulders when a whisper of movement warned him he was not alone. He spun as an apparition shambled out of the darkness and flung widespread arms around him. His fist rose but he did not finish the swing.

"Fargo?" William Peel blurted, and collapsed, the feathered end of an arrow protruding from his shirt midway down.

Fargo caught him and eased Peel onto his back. He did not need to inspect the wound to know it would prove fatal. The barbed tip had sheared through Peel's lung and ruptured out his back to the left of his spine. As if to confirm it, Peal suffered a violent coughing fit that ended with dark drops flecking his lips.

"Water," Peel rasped. "I need water."

"I don't have any," Fargo said.

"It's just not my day." Peel gripped the arrow and feebly tugged. "Help me pull this out."

"You'll die that much sooner," Fargo informed him.

"Die? Me?" Peel was stunned. "I can't die. Not now. Not when I'm so close. Peelville is just over these hills."

"Tell me about the Sioux."

"There were four of them. They came out of no-where and put arrows into Clements and me before we could get off a shot. Maxton and the rest fled, the cowards, and I made it up here in the confusion." Peel tugged on the shaft anyway, resulting in another fit of coughing.

"I hear Maxton has your journal," Fargo said.

"That bastard," Peel wheezed. "The extra money I was going to give him wasn't enough. He has to have it all."

"Extra money?"

"To dispose of the others once I had the chest," Peel said without thinking. "I wasn't about to share it with my cousins. They were a means to an end, nothing more." He laughed but it came out as a strangled gurgle. "Tom and all his talk about family. He was always too trusting."

"So you planned to betray them, and instead, Maxton betrayed you." Fargo thought it fitting.

"You can't trust anyone anymore."

Fargo slid his right hand into his pocket but he did not draw the derringer. *Why waste the bullet?* he asked himself.

"My only consolation is that Amanda won't get her hands on the chest, either," Peel was saying. "The bitch. Serves her right."

"I don't understand," Fargo admitted.

"She was in this with me," Peel said irritably. "We were to split the treasure between us. All that bull she fed me about undying love and devotion! I should have known better."

"You and your cousin?"

Peel clutched at him. "Don't let Maxton get away with this. The chest is in the basement of the big house my great uncle was having built. In the northwest corner, three feet underground. It should be easy to find. Kill Maxton and it's all yours, all the wealth you would

129

ever want. I just wish I could be there to see his face. I just wish—" Whatever else William Peel wished was lost with the fading vestige of his life. The most violent fit yet seized him, and when it was over, the betrayer was no more.

Fargo had a wish of his own. He wished Peel had suffered more.

16

Fargo was rounding a hill when he startled three untended horses. Two were pack animals laden with packs. They bolted, making enough racket to attract every Sioux in the vicinity. The third horse, though, whinnied and trotted up to him and nuzzled his chest with genuine affection.

"I've missed you," Fargo told the Ovaro, and patted its neck. He snatched the dangling reins and stepped to the saddle. The cinch was loose but otherwise everything was as it should be; his saddlebags had not been touched, his bedroll was intact, and, wonder of wonders, the Henry was in the scabbard.

Fargo shucked it and worked the lever, and yes, it was loaded. *Why didn't Maxton or one of his men help themselves?* he wondered, and shrugged. Their mistake had given him a fighting chance to make it out of Dakota Territory alive. He shoved the Henry back in, adjusted the cinch, forked leather, and was off, riding hard after the pack animals. They had not gone far. Neither spooked as he came alongside and gathered up their lead ropes.

Peel had told him the ghost town was to the north of the hills, so it was to the north that Fargo gigged the stallion. Only six of the original group were left: Thomas, Amanda, Monique, Maxton, Trint and Ames. If any were still alive, that was where they would head.

Fargo had tried to warn them. Again and again he

had advised against their quest. But they refused to listen. They thought they knew better. They figured he was exaggerating the perils. Now look. He supposed he shouldn't blame them, though. To many pampered Easterners, civilized sorts who could go their entire lives without once having their lives threatened, the notion that there were people who would kill them without batting an eye or wild beasts that considered them two-legged feasts was a hard fact to grasp. They tended to think it couldn't happen to them. That no one would ever *really* try to snuff out their wick. That a bear or wolf wouldn't *really* relish eating them. Too often, they learned the truth too late.

A yellow glow brought an end to Fargo's reverie. He was out of the hills, and ahead lay a fork of the stream they had been following. He forded it and scaled a short bank on the other side.

Woodland confronted him. Oaks and cottonwoods and willows. Fargo quietly slid the Henry out and rested it across his saddle. A light tap of his spurs goaded the Ovaro forward.

The glow came from a lantern sitting on the ground, unattended. Fargo drew rein and waited for whoever put it there to show themselves. But minutes went by and no one appeared. Puzzled, he circled to the right. When he had gone a short way he saw a pair of boots at the fringe of light.

Sliding down, Fargo looped the reins and the lead ropes around low limbs, then crept closer. It was Ames, belly down, his throat slit from ear to ear. He had tried to draw his pistol but he was dead before he hit the ground. The pool of blood under his body was almost dry.

Fargo picked up the lantern. Tracks and scuff marks left clues to Ames' final moments. Maxton had snuck up behind him and done the deed, then stood and watched Ames bleed out. He had gone on alone, on foot.

There was no end to the betrayals. Now that Maxton believed they almost had the treasure chest within their grasp, he was killing his own men. He wanted it all for himself. How he hoped to get it past the Sioux was a question he probably hadn't considered. Greed tended to blind the greedy to reality.

Fargo blew out the lantern and left it there. He would come back for it later, if he could. He returned to the horses but didn't untie the pack animals. They would keep, too.

A hundred yards farther the woods thinned. Fargo reined up yet again, the Henry's stock to his shoulder. A vague shape had materialized out of the undergrowth. Something about it made him think he should know what it was, but it wasn't until he came within a few yards that the truth dawned, and what it signified. He had found Peelville. Or where Peelville had stood.

The crumpled remains of a stone fireplace and chimney thrust a blunt column at the night sky. Fargo was careful not to get too close. From the way it was leaning, it wouldn't take much for the whole thing to come crashing down.

Fargo looked around for signs of the floor and walls but there was just the fireplace, nothing more. That made no sense. Dismounting, he crisscrossed the area around it but could find no other trace of the structure the fireplace had been part of. Mystified, he wheeled toward the pinto and his boot struck a long object, partially buried.

Hunkering, Fargo ran a hand over it. When he removed the hand, his palm and fingers were black. It was a timber. A charred, weatherworn timber that once might have supported a wall or a ceiling.

Fargo wiped his hand on his leggings and climbed back on the Ovaro. Another light caught his eye. This one was moving, flitting back and forth like a bright yellow moth. He rode cautiously toward it.

The person holding the lantern was frantically scouring the ground. "It has to be here! It has to!" he was saying over and over again.

Fargo brought the stallion to a stop ten yards out and leveled the Henry. "You'll never find it."

Maxton stopped and turned but did not grab for the revolver on his hip. "What are you talking about? It's here! I know it's here." He held out his other hand. In it was a small leather-bound volume. "Benedict Peel's journal says so! You can read the entries for yourself."

"I don't need to."

"The old pirate had no reason to lie," Maxton said, his voice oddly high-pitched. "The treasure chest was real. He brought it with him and buried it in the house he was building."

"I'm sure he did," Fargo agreed. "But you still won't find it."

Gazing about in bewilderment, Maxton said plaintively, "Don't you understand? I *have* to find it. I've come too far. Done too much."

"I found Ames," Fargo said.

Maxton did not seem to hear him. "This is the chance of a lifetime. I'll be rich! You hear me? Rich as rich can be." He took a step to the right, then another to the left. "All I have to do is find it. All I have to do is figure out where Peel's house stood."

"You never will."

"Why do you keep saying that?" Maxton cried. "Who's going to stop me? You? The Stains? The stinking Sioux?"

"The land," Fargo said.

Maxton dismissed the idea with a gesture of contempt. "You're crazy. What does the land have to do with anything?"

"Lafitte was run out of Galveston in 1821. Benedict Peel came north not long after that. Which means it's been forty years, Maxton. Forty years since the Sioux ran him off and burned Peelville down. Forty years for the vegetation to grow and the land to erase nearly every trace of the town. The streets, the buildings, they're almost all gone."

"There are a few signs left," Maxton stubbornly insisted. "I saw a fireplace earlier. All I have to do is wait for the sun to come up and I'll find the chest in no time."

"Provided you live that long."

Maxton swung around and shook the journal at him. "So that's how it is? You plan to kill me and take the journal so you can have all the treasure for yourself."

"I'm going to kill you because you tried to kill me, you son of a bitch," Fargo responded.

"That's just an excuse!" Maxton's eyes had a wild gleam to them, and his mouth was twitching. "But don't do anything hasty! We can be partners. We'll split the chest fifty-fifty. Equal shares. What do you say?"

"Like the share you gave Ames?"

"He wanted the treasure for himself, just like the rest. I had to kill him before he killed me."

"Where are Thomas and Amanda?"

"How should I know? We scattered when the Sioux jumped us. We had stopped to rest and most of us had dismounted, and our damn horses ran off. The last I saw of those two, they were running like hell. He couldn't manage on his own so she was helping him."

"Monique?"

Maxton shrugged. "Things were happening too fast for me to keep track of everyone."

Fargo had one last question. "And my Colt?"

"Trint has it. He was the only one still in the saddle and took off like a bat out of a cave." Maxton's eyes narrowed. "I see you got your hands on your rifle. That pinto of yours wouldn't let us touch it. Every time we went near your saddle, it reared and kicked."

Fargo curled his finger around the Henry's trigger. "You can put down the lantern if you want."

"Damned decent of you," Maxton said with more

than a trace of sarcasm. "You're a strange one, mister. If I were in your place, I'd have shot me in the back when I rode up. Why didn't you?"

"I want you to see it coming," Fargo said.

"We never know, do we? When it's our time? And nothing we do or say can prevent it." Maxton held the lantern out from his side but he didn't set it down. "This hasn't turned out as I thought it would."

He was stalling, and Fargo could guess why. "Pompey would say the same thing if he were still alive. You remember him, don't you? The man you gunned down when he tried to help me."

"You're upset over a darky? Hell, they're hardly human. Besides, he wasn't of any use to me."

"Why did you shoot Emma Stain?"

"She went crazy. I was about to put a slug into you for good measure after Trint hit you and she came at me like a madwoman, clawing at my face and eyes. I had to kill her or she would have blinded me. Then her brother acted up and I winged him to keep him in line. By then I was so mad, I made them mount up and we left."

"Leaving me for the vultures."

"Vultures, hell. With all that blood, I thought you were dead. So did Trint. Your head must be made of iron." Maxton paused. "Well, I guess we've said all that needs saying. Let's get this over with."

"Light the fuse," Fargo said.

They stared at one another, Fargo waiting for Maxton to drop the lantern and the journal and go for his revolver, and Maxton tensing for his final play. It was then, in the deep silence, with the only sound the sigh of the breeze, that a slender shaft streaked out of nowhere and transfixed Maxton from back to front high on his left side. The jolt staggered him but he didn't collapse and didn't cry out.

Another arrow whisked past Fargo's ear as he shifted and fired at shadows rushing from the trees. A warrior spun completely around, then fell. Two others were nocking shafts to sinew bow strings.

Fargo slapped his legs and the Ovaro bounded into the darkness. Twisting, he banged off another shot but missed.

Maxton had dropped the lantern and drawn his revolver. Clutching his shoulder, he squeezed off three shots while backpedaling into the brush.

Then Fargo was in the clear, or thought he was. Another painted Sioux loomed directly in his path, and a stout arm rose to hurl a lance. Fargo's Henry boomed. The warrior swayed but still managed to hurl the lance. Ducking, Fargo passed under it while reining sharply to the left. He heard Maxton's revolver crack twice. After that, all was quiet.

When he had gone far enough for it to be reasonably safe, Fargo drew rein. None of the Sioux had given chase. Since he wouldn't be of much help to Monique or the Stains blundering around in the dark, he alighted and led the Ovaro into the blackest patch of shadow he could find. His back to a willow and the cocked Henry in his lap, he waited for dawn.

It was a long time coming. Twice he heard rustling that might or might not be the Sioux. Later a scream shattered the deceptive stillness. Whether it was a woman or a man, he couldn't tell.

The eastern sky brightened. When it was light enough that Fargo could distinguish leaves and blades of grass, he mounted and rode west, then south, avoiding the townsite, or what was left of it. He was close to the hills when another scream rose from among them. This time there was no mistaking—it was a man.

Fargo rode up the nearest hill to within twenty feet of the crest. To avoid silhouetting himself against the rising sun, he crawled to the top and peered over. They were down there, all right, five Sioux and a captive. They had stripped him naked and staked him out, spreadeagle. Now they were hunkered around him, poking him with their knives and lances, amusing themselves.

Broken Horn was not one of the five.

Sighting down the Henry, Fargo centered the sights on a warrior holding a bone-handled knife. Before he could shoot, the Sioux sliced it into the captive, and twisted it. Another scream echoed among the hills, causing every bird within earshot to take wing.

"You wouldn't listen," Fargo said, and fired.

The warrior leaped erect, flung a hand to his chest, and toppled. Instantly the other four scrambled for their horses. Only two made it. Hanging from the sides of their mounts, they fled beyond the next hill.

Fargo thought they might circle to come at him from the rear but the next time he saw them, they were a quarter of a mile to the south, riding hard. He climbed on the Ovaro and warily descended. One of the Sioux was still moving, a situation remedied by a bullet to the brain.

The captive was still alive. He had been partially skinned and partially scalped. His ears were gone and his nose had been cut off. So had the fingers on his left hand and the toes on his left foot. As if that were not enough, he had been stabbed several times but not in his vitals so he would live longer. Bloodshot lidless eyes were raised to Fargo as he rode up.

"Kill me," Thomas Stain begged.

17

The memory would live with Fargo for a long time. Climbing down, palming the Toothpick as he sank onto a knee. Asking Stain if he knew where Monique and Amanda were.

"I'm sorry. I don't. Amanda left me to go for water and the Sioux found me before she came back." Tears trickled down Thomas's cheek. "End it. Now. Please. I can't take much more."

"I'm sorry."

"For what? I'm the one who knew it all. I'm the one who fell for William's lies and brought my brother and sisters out here to die." Thomas uttered a choking sob. "I deserve this. I deserve worse. If you see Amanda, tell her I was thinking about her at the end. She was always the one I trusted most."

Fargo thought of William Peel. "I won't rest until I find her."

"Please," Stain said. "Please."

A quick flick of Fargo's wrist sufficed. He wiped the doubled-edged blade clean on the grass. Only four were left, and if he had his way, three more would be a pile of bleached bones come spring.

He trotted east along the hills until he came to a ravine and a lone frail figure caked with dirt and grime, her hair disheveled, her uniform a travesty of its former impeccable luster, on her knees near it. Her hands were clasped as if she were in prayer, and tears smudged her face. She shook her head as he came to a stop and said "No!" as he swung down and placed his hands on her shoulders.

"Are you all right, Monique?"

"Oh, handsome one! He has you now."

"Who does?" Fargo suspected the truth before Trint stepped from the mouth of the ravine with Fargo's own Colt pointed at him.

"Don't so much as twitch." Trint smirked in triumph. "I didn't think it would be this easy. Using her as bait worked fine."

"I am sorry," Monique said to Fargo. "He made me do it. He hurt me, bad."

"I couldn't risk winging you and have you get away," Trint said. "I had to get you in close so I could be certain. Now suppose you drop that rifle, nice and slow, and step back from the cute little miss. Your hands where I can see them, if you don't mind."

"One shot will bring the Sioux down on your head," Fargo mentioned as he released the Henry.

"Nice try, but they don't worry me. Not now that I have your horse and mine to ride in relays. They'll never catch me. I'll be back at Foy's Landing inside the week, and on the next steamboat downriver."

Fargo stepped back, his hands in front of him, close to his waist. "What about the treasure chest?"

"I value my life more. And Maxton is still out there somewhere. Maxton, with all his talk about how he would steal the treasure right out from under Peel and the Stains, and then it would be share and share alike." Trint swore lustily. "Share, my ass. I saw him kill Ames. I was next, only I didn't stick around. I outsmarted the bastard, and now I've outsmarted you."

Fargo moved his right hand a fraction of an inch. "You don't need to worry about Maxton anymore. The last I saw of him, he had a Sioux arrow in his shoulder."

"You don't say?" Trint laughed. "It couldn't happen to a nicer backstabber."

Fargo nodded at Monique, who was quaking with fear. "What about her? Don't let the Sioux get their hands on her."

"Why should I care? She's nothing to me. They can scalp her or throw her off a cliff if they want."

Monique started to stand but thought better of it. "You are despicable, *monsieur*. Worse than the red men. They hate us because we invade their land. What is your excuse?"

"I don't need one," Trint mocked her. "You mean nothing to me, lady. The rest of you can go to the devil, and good riddance." He raised the Colt a little higher. "I guess you know what's next," he told Fargo.

"One of us dies and one of us lives."

"*You* die. *I* live." Trint sidled toward the Ovaro. "Don't worry about your horse. I might even keep it for myself."

"One last question," Fargo said.

"Make it quick. I don't have all damn day."

Fargo drew the derringer and shot Trint in the forehead so quickly that Trint was dead before his brain could command his finger to tighten on the Colt. The body lurched to the right like a puppet whose strings had suddenly been cut. Three short steps, muscles working in reflex, and Trint melted like wax.

Monique jumped at the shot. Her hand flew to her throat, then her arms were around Fargo and she was sobbing into his chest. "Take me away from this terrible place! All the killing! All the blood! Horror after horror!"

"Monique—"

"*S'il vous plaît!* I beg you! Or I will lose my sanity!"

Fargo was going to say that he had Maxton and Amanda to deal with yet, but the panic in Monique's eyes convinced him she truly was on the verge of snapping. "You can ride Trint's horse."

To avoid the Sioux, Fargo traveled well to the east of the hills, then on around to the stream, to the sheltered glade they had camped in before. A fire might give them away so they made do with jerky from his saddlebags. Hardly had he spread out his bedroll than Monique was curled on her side, sound asleep. He stayed up another hour, listening. Shortly before he turned in he thought he heard hooves but if so it was only one horse and it was nowhere near them.

The next morning, Monique did not want to wake up. He had to shake her several times before she stirred, and then she complained that she was too tired to ride. "We should rest another day, *chéri*."

"If that's what you want," Fargo said. "Just don't blame me if the Sioux find us."

Monique changed her mind. She was ready, after all.

The vegetation along the stream was the perfect cover. Fargo never rode in the open, even for short distances. About ten o'clock a cloud of dust a mile off gave him cause for concern. A large group of riders were heading toward the hills. More Sioux, he reckoned.

At midday Fargo halted. He brought the Ovaro to the water's edge to drink, and as he stood there debating which route would see them safely to the Missouri River, he noticed hoofprints on a gravel bar. Prints made by a shod horse.

Monique noticed him studying them. "What is it?"

"Two people on one horse, riding down the middle of the stream to throw off the Sioux. One of the two is hurt. Their horse is tired, and unless they rest soon, they'll ride it into the ground." Fargo touched a muddy print. "About an hour ahead of us, maybe less."

"You can tell all that? Even that one is hurt?"

"See these red drops? It's blood." Fargo had a fair idea who the hurt rider must be.

"Whoever they are, we want nothing to do with them. Right?"

"Wrong." Fargo was not one to forgive and forget. Turning the other cheek was for those who didn't mind being filled with lead or gutted by cold steel. He had an aversion to both.

"I don't like the way you say that," Monique said. "Hasn't there been enough killing?"

"Not with Maxton still alive."

"So what if he is?"

"Maxton killed Emma and Elizabeth. Maxton killed Pompey. Maxton planned to kill all of you and keep the treasure for himself."

"Again, so? What does that have to do with us? We are alive. We can leave this terrible land." Monique put a hand on his arm. "Let us leave him be and go."

"If he makes it back, no one will ever know what he did. He won't be arrested or go on trial. He'll have gotten away with murder."

"We can report him to the authorities," Monique proposed. "Let them deal with him."

"It would be his word against ours," Fargo said. "And no one has jurisdiction out here."

"The military, then?"

"The army doesn't get involved in civilian matters except in special cases," Fargo set her straight. "It doesn't go around arresting people." He shook his head. "No, the only ones who can punish Maxton for what he's done are you and me."

"There must be another way. I have no desire to punish him. Only to leave this behind me and never think of it again."

"Then it's up to me." Fargo straightened.

"You are not a lawman." Monique refused to let it drop. "You have no legal authority."

"I have this." Fargo patted the Colt.

"But you can't set yourself up as judge and jury. You can't kill everyone who does wrong. If all of us did that, what would the world be like?"

"If no one does it, the Maxtons take over. The only thing that keeps men like him from doing what they please is that they know someone somewhere will stand up to them. Someone will stop them. Someone *must* stop them."

"Please," Monique said, grasping the front of his buckskin shirt. "No more. For me, *oui*?"

"How about if we leave it up to Maxton?" Fargo suggested.

That was where they left it until an hour and a half later when they spied a weary horse trudging down the middle of the stream. Fargo had been right about the dripping blood; Maxton was one of the two riders. The other one surprised him. Both were slumped over, Maxton weakened by his wound, the other one from exhaustion. Neither heard the Ovaro until it was a few yards behind them. Then Maxton stiffened and clawed at the revolver at his hip, crying, "They've found us!"

Fargo already had his Colt out. "I wouldn't," he said, coming up next to them and pointing the Colt at Maxton's head.

"No!" Maxton jerked his hand into the air. "Don't shoot! I thought you were Sioux!" He was pale and haggard. The arrow had been removed and a crude bandage applied, consisting of strips cut from the bottom of his shirt.

Amanda Stain held the reins. She brought their horse to a stop and tiredly smiled, "Fargo! Monique! Thank God the two of you are all right."

"Your cousin sends his regards," Fargo said coldly.

"William?" Amanda said, acting as if she did not understand. "He's alive, too? Where is he?"

"No, he's dead," Fargo said, "but before he died, he told me how the two of you were going to keep the treasure for yourselves."

"What?" Maxton said.

"What?" Monique echoed.

Amanda laughed but her eyes were troubled. "That's preposterous. Turn against my brothers and sisters? If Tom were here, he would tell you I'd never do anything like that."

"Tom is dead, too," Fargo said. "You're the last Stain left." Leaning over, he relieved Maxton of the revolver and stuck it under his belt. Amanda wasn't armed. "Keep riding. But don't try anything."

"What do you intend to do with us?" Maxton asked.

"According to Monique, there's not much I can do," Fargo answered. To Amanda he said, "How is it the two of you are together?"

"I was separated from the rest when the Sioux attacked," she explained. "I was wandering in the dark, scared out of my wits, when I heard someone coming. It was Maxton. He had an arrow in his shoulder. I helped pull it out and bandaged him. Then we found this horse, and here we are."

"You helped the man who murdered your sisters?"

"Maxton had a gun. I didn't. He was my best hope of getting out alive," Amanda justified herself. "Don't make more of it than there is."

By late afternoon they were miles from the hills. Monique was asleep, her cheek on Fargo's shoulder blade, her arms loosely wrapped around his waist. Maxton dozed fitfully. Once when he awoke he asked if he could climb down and soak his wound but Fargo wouldn't let him. "Not until nightfall. Until I'm sure we're safe."

An hour before sunset Monique stirred. She sat up and smacked her lips and said in his ear, "How soon before we stop? I'm sore all over."

"Not long," Fargo said. He heard a sharp intake of breath, and twisting, gazed back as she was doing. Through a gap in the trees riders were visible, strung out in single file and coming on fast.

"Indians!" Monique exclaimed.

Fargo spurred the Ovaro alongside Amanda and Maxton. "We're not out of this yet. Four Sioux are on our trail."

"How can they follow us? We're in the middle of the stream. We're not leaving any tracks," Amanda marveled.

"Look again," Fargo said. Because they *were* leaving tracks. The water washed away some but not all, and every step their horses took raised mud from the bottom, turning the stream brown. The wonder of it was that it had taken the Sioux this long to find them.

"What do we do?" Amanda asked.

"We make a stand," Fargo said. They had no choice. They couldn't outrun them.

Maxton held out his hand. "Give back my revolver. You'll need help."

The hell of it was, he was right. Fargo couldn't do it alone. Although a tiny voice deep in the recesses of his mind screamed at him not to, he did as Maxton wanted. "After you," he said to Amanda, nodding at the bank. She reined up it and he promptly followed.

They did not have much time. Five minutes, if that.

"I don't want to die," Monique declared.

"Who does?" Fargo said. But they soon might.

18

Broken Horn was in the lead. He now had a rifle, taken from one of Maxton's men, and a revolver strapped around his waist, butt forward. Two of the three warriors with him also had rifles.

From his place of concealment, crouched behind a tree on the north bank, Fargo waited for them to round the last bend. His hat was on the ground beside him. Several feet away, behind another tree, Maxton squatted, nervously fingering his revolver.

Fargo hadn't counted on the Sioux having guns. He should have expected it, though. His fatigue was to blame. He wasn't as sharp, mentally or physically, as he should be. Neither was Maxton. They were no match for four well-armed and alert Sioux. They would need luck to come out on top. Lots and lots of luck.

Broken Horn rounded the bend and immediately reined up. He regarded the stretch of stream ahead suspiciously. He was wily, this one, with the instincts of a natural predator, and he sensed something was amiss.

"Don't shoot until I do," Fargo whispered.

Maxton glanced at him but did not say anything. From the way he was twitching, Fargo could only hope he didn't do something rash.

The other three warriors had stopped behind Broken Horn. They would not move until he did.

Fargo thought of Monique and Amanda, hidden back among the trees. He had told them to keep the horses quiet, and if he yelled, they were to mount up and ride for their lives.

Broken Horn kneed his warhorse and came on at a walk, glancing from one bank to the other, watching the woods, not the stream.

Maxton raised his revolver, then lowered it again. He was chewing on his lower lip and his face was slick with sweat.

Fargo held the Henry vertical, close to the oak. He had to wait to take aim until the Sioux were so close he couldn't miss. Otherwise, the gleam of the brass might give him away.

Broken Horn slowed. He was almost to the spot where they had all gone up the north bank but he was staring at the trees on the south side.

Maxton was fidgeting worse than ever. He thumbed back the revolver's hammer and then let it down. There was a distinct *click*.

Fargo glanced at Broken Horn. The young warrior had heard but he was not sure where the sound came from. Broken Horn looked north; he looked south; he tucked his rifle to his side. Fargo took a breath and held it. The time to act was now, before the Sioux could break for cover. He leaned out, whipped the Henry to his shoulder, and took a hasty bead. But as fast as he was, Broken Horn was faster. The warrior dived off his horse and was up the south bank in a blur.

Fargo fired and saw the slug kick earth into the air. He levered in another round but by then Broken Horn had sought cover. Swiveling, Fargo aimed at a Sioux charging straight at them. Maxton's revolver barked and the Sioux was knocked halfway around but he kept on coming, spraying lead. Fargo's shot cored his torso and the warrior thudded onto his back and didn't move.

The other two had left the stream farther down. Bent low, they were almost to the vegetation when Maxton triggered two swift shots. One of the Sioux mounts squealed and tumbled into a forward roll, throwing its rider.

Fargo lost sight of them. He moved to a different tree and motioned for Maxton to do the same but Maxton was reloading and talking to himself out loud.

"Teach those red devils! See if we don't! They're not taking my scalp! No sir! Do you hear me, you filthy savages?"

"Quiet," Fargo whispered.

"Not getting me!" Maxton cackled. "There's still hope. We'll come back with more men and search until we find it. Enough men to hold off every last Sioux in all of creation."

Fargo didn't warn him again. Maxton could dig his own grave if he wanted. In fact, Fargo was glad Maxton wouldn't listen. Dropping onto his side, he wormed his way around a bush so he had a clear view of where the two warriors on the north side of the stream had disappeared.

"Come and get it, you vermin!" Maxton shouted. "Come and get a taste of your own medicine! Put an arrow in me, will you? I'll show you. I'll show every one of you heathen sons of bitches."

The vegetation parted and out they bounded, one firing a rifle from the hip, the other unleashing arrow after arrow. Howling like rabid wolves, they were on Maxton before he could turn. A shaft pierced his side, a slug struck him in the neck. Maxton fired but his legs were giving way and both shots were high.

Fargo didn't shoot. He could have. He had clear shots. But he waited until an arrow tore into Maxton's throat and a slug slammed into his ribs. Only then did Fargo fire, two rapid shots, going for their heads. At each blast a Sioux fell.

In the sudden silence Maxton's thrashing was unnaturally loud. He whined and gagged and raised a clawed hand toward the sky, and died.

Fargo changed position again. Motionless, he waited. Broken Horn was out there and Broken Horn was the most dangerous.

Sparrows chirped and frolicked. A squirrel went from tree to tree along the thin limbs of the upper terrace. A fly droned around for a while but flew off.

Fargo hoped the two women had the good sense to stay put. The only thing to do was wait Broken Horn out, and that could take the rest of the day.

Suddenly foliage ten yards to the right parted, framing a swarthy visage. Fargo slowly started to take aim but Broken Horn melted into the greenery. He trained the Henry on the spot hoping Broken Horn would reappear but after five minutes he knew it was pointless.

Another fly, or maybe it was the same one, buzzed his head and shoulders. Fargo was tempted to swat it but he stayed still. It landed on his left ear and he foolishly gave a toss of his head to get it to go elsewhere. Almost instantly a rifle spanged and a slug smacked into the tree next to him. He threw himself down and to the left. The rifle boomed again and invisible fingers plucked at the whangs on his sleeve. Then he was on his belly in a shallow depression, safe for the moment, but that would change as soon as Broken Horn worked around for a clear shot.

Fargo hurtled up and out and into a patch of high brush. A rifle cracked and lead missed him by a whisker. He went to ground as the space above him was peppered.

As before, quiet descended. Fargo's chin was on his forearm and he was in no hurry to move. He would let Broken Horn worry awhile about whether he was still there.

There had not been a peep out of the women. Ordinarily that would be reassuring but Fargo grew strangely troubled. Amanda and Monique were not frontier stock. They were city bred, and it had been his experience that city dwellers couldn't sit still for very long even when their lives were at stake. He would have thought one of them would call out to see if he was all right, or come investigate for themselves.

Fargo's unease grew. He tried to tell himself he was being silly, that he should be grateful the women had done as he told them. But it didn't feel right. Without lifting his head, he crawled to the right until he had gone far enough to rise onto his knees without being shot at. Or so he hoped. He had a few tense moments as he unfurled, then he was tucked at the waist and winding through the undergrowth.

Suddenly a rifle boomed, so close that the smoke from the muzzle blast wreathed Fargo's face and its acrid odor filled his nose. He thought he had been shot but there was no pain. Throwing himself to one side, he saw Broken Horn only a few feet away. How the Sioux missed, Fargo had no idea, unless in his excitement Broken Horn has rushed his shot. Now the young warrior was frantically trying to feed a fresh cartridge into the chamber of his rifle. Only, the rifle was jammed.

Fargo brought the Henry up to shoot. Growling deep in his throat, Broken Horn reversed his grip and attacked, wielding the rifle like a club. Fargo dodged the first swing but the second caught the Henry across the barrel, knocking it from his hands. Springing in close, he grabbed Broken Horn's rifle to prevent Broken Horn from swinging again.

Struggling to gain the upper hand, they spun this way and that.

Fargo nearly wrested it free but Broken Horn clung on. Another spin, and Fargo slammed into a cottonwood. His shoulder jarred with pain. He braced his legs and spun Broken Horn around, and the young Sioux stumbled and lost his grip. Broken Horn pitched to his knees, steadied himself, and went for the knife at his waist instead of the revolver. Maybe he forgot he had it. Or maybe he went for the knife out of habit. Whichever the case, as the blade flashed from its sheath, Fargo drew his Colt. He fired as the knife lanced at his groin, fired as Broken Horn recoiled, fired as the Sioux heaved erect and stabbed at his throat, then emptied the Colt into the twitching body at his feet.

The blasts rippled off across the prairie. Fargo reloaded, reclaimed the Henry, and rolled the warrior over. Broken Horn's days of killing were over.

Fargo went to the Sioux with the bow and took it and the quiver for his own. Then he hurried toward where he had left the women. "It's all right!" he hollered to soothe their fears. "We're safe now." He pushed through chest-high weeds and stopped in consternation. The Ovaro and the other horse were gone. "Monique?" he shouted. "Where are you?" He figured they had fled. They couldn't take the strain of waiting and by now they were hell-bent for the Missouri River.

Fargo stopped and pushed his hat back on his head. He wasn't mad. But he didn't like the prospect of the long walk ahead of him. Starting to turn, he saw a shoe. A female shoe, the kind he once slid off certain shapely female feet. "Monique?"

She was belly down, her leg crooked at an odd angle. His blood chilling, Fargo dashed to her side and rolled her over. "Monique," he said softly, horrified by her wide, lifeless eyes, and the rope around her neck. She had been strangled. Cruelly, deliberately strangled. Broken, bloody fingernails testified to the fight she had put up.

Fargo searched for footprints and found only one other set where the struggle had been fiercest. For a long time he just stood there. Then he roused himself and dug a grave. It wasn't as deep as he would like but it would have to do.

The tracks of the two horses pointed south. She was leading the Ovaro and riding the other one.

Fargo jogged the first hundred yards. Thereafter, he walked at a pace so brisk, only an Apache could match it. For a while he was numb inside. Numb to the world, numb to his feelings, numb to everything except his burning thirst for vengeance, a thirst that drove him during the long afternoon and long after the sun went down.

He didn't think about what he would do when he caught her. If she were a man he would walk up to her, give her a chance to go for her pistol, and shoot her dead. But she was a woman and he could never do to a woman what he would do to a man unless the woman was about to take his life.

Midnight. One in the morning. Two. Fargo's calves were cramping when he stopped. He curled up right where he was, placed the Henry and the bow and the quiver next to him, and within moments was asleep.

Sunrise found him already on the move. He had gone about a mile when he saw both horses grazing near the stream. She had not bothered to strip off their saddles. He heard her light snores before he saw her. She was under a tree, bundled in blankets. He stood looking down at her, then poked her with a toe. "Wake up, Amanda."

She came out from under the blankets in a mad scramble. Racing to the other horse, she galloped off into the woods, her hair streaming behind her.

Fargo made no move to give chase. There was no need. He saw something she didn't. "Amanda!" he shouted. "You shouldn't have!"

Amanda Stain straightened and twisted and sneered in contempt. She still had not noticed the oak with the low limb. "Go to hell!" she yelled, and threw back her head and laughed.

The *crack* of her neck breaking was sharp and clear.

Oscar Foy lumbered out of his trading post and stretched. He moved toward his dugout, scratching himself. The setting sun was in his eyes and he did not notice Fargo until Fargo said his name. Whirling, Foy placed his hand on his pistol. "What in hell? You!"

"Me," Fargo said.

"What are you doing with that thing?" Foy demanded.

"What does it look like?"

The trader's piglet eyes glittered hatred. "Why? I'm entitled to know that much, aren't I?"

"They're all dead," Fargo said. "Every last one."

"What does that have to do with me?" Foy blustered. "I've been here the whole time."

"I know you have," Fargo said.

"Then how can you blame it on me?" Foy smugly demanded.

"Broken Horn."

"What about him?"

"I saw the two of you together," Fargo explained, and drew the arrow back another half an inch, stretching the bow taut.

"Oh," Foy said. He glanced up and down the river but there were no boats coming, and then at the trading post door, but it was too far to reach. "I don't suppose you would take money?"

Fargo held the bow steady.

"Five hundred, say? Or how about a thousand? You forget what you saw and we go our own ways."

"Whenever you're ready to die," Fargo said.

"I get it. You think you're clever. When they find me with the arrow in my chest, they'll blame the Sioux."

"Not one arrow. The whole quiver."

Oscar Foy stared at the barbed point. "Just so you know, you bastard, I'd do it the same if I had it to do all over again." He shook his left fist as a distraction, his right swooping to his Smith and Wesson.

The bow string twanged eleven times.

Fargo opened the corral and shooed the horses out so they could fend for themselves. He went into the trading post and helped himself to a few items. Then he climbed on the Ovaro, rode upriver a ways, and threw the bow and the quiver in the water. "What do you say to a week to ourselves over in the Rockies?" he asked the stallion as he headed west. "I can use the peace and quiet."

*Utah Territory, 1859—where the profit-and-
loss ledgers are written in blood, and Fargo
is keeping accounts.*

"We won't die," the pretty brunette announced in a
voice rubbed raw by thirst and grit. "A stranger is
coming. A tall man who has no more fear in him than
a rifle."

"Yes," snapped John Beckmann, her brother-in-
law, "and every Jack shall have his Jill, too. *No one*
is going to ride in and save us, Dora. This is real life,
not some penny dreadful."

They were crossing a vast desert plain between
scarred ranges of sterile mountains. The wind-driven
grit felt like buckshot, and a blazing yellow sun was
stuck high in the sky as if pegged there. Alkali dust

hung curtain-thick in the air, the searing sunlight turning it into a blinding white haze.

"The gateway to California," Beckmann said bitterly even as he staggered and almost fell. He was a thin, intelligent-looking, sickly man dressed in sober black. "This is all my fault. In all the blowing dust, I fear I missed the place where the California Trail veers west from the Bear River. Like a fool, I swore by the Hastings guidebook as if it were Scripture. I—"

"John, there's no point in repeating all that," gently admonished his wife, Estelline, who was at least seven months along with child.

But Beckmann didn't seem to hear her. "No way to fight shy of the southern route through the Utah deserts, that infernal book insists, if we wish to avoid being caught by snow in the Sierras. I should have asked others. Now look—I've killed my own family!"

One of the children, four-year-old Lloyd, began crying, and wearily John picked up the exhausted boy. Three more small children trudged through the salt-desert waste.

"We're all still very much alive, John," Estelline managed bravely. "But our mouths feel stuffed with cotton."

"No water since yesterday, that's why. Not to mention your empty bellies, rock-torn feet, and going half blind from the cursed glare," John replied.

It broke his heart to see Estelline, Dora, and the little ones trudging through this hellish landscape afoot. What sorry grass he'd found was so salt-encrusted the stock couldn't eat it. Deliberately poisoned water holes hastened the deaths of their yoke oxen and butcher beef.

"I was fully prepared to see my school in Los Angeles fail," he admitted. "The place is a lick-skittle settlement. But I always believed we'd at least make it out there—"

"We'll make it because help is coming," Dora insisted again. She held up a round crystal glass mounted in a glazed porcelain base. "My peeping stone never lies."

"Miracles, I believe in," Beckmann muttered. "But not devil-inspired sorcery."

"Doesn't matter if you believe," she replied. "Miracle or magic, a tall stranger *is* coming. And water with him."

Dora was pretty and petite like her older sister Estelline. She had lively green eyes and mother-of-pearl skin. Despite their desperate situation, her jet-black hair hung in two long braids tied with white ribbons in front of each shoulder. Her flowered muslin dress had been pretty before the salt dust coated it.

Beckmann cast a baleful glance around, his eyes trembling and watering—the salt-desert hardpan produced a glare that could drive animals and humans mad. Back east, Salt Lake was being called "the Half Way House" between the Missouri River and the Pacific Ocean. All he'd found, so far, was a harsh, unforgiving land of tarantulas, centipedes, and scorpions. In this desolate salt-desert waste, no joyous birds celebrated sunup. It was an arid land of *borrasca,* barren rock.

A land of the dead. And soon—perhaps even within hours now—his own family's bones would be bleaching among the rest.

A worried Skye Fargo sleeved sweat out of his eyes, wondering if he and the Ovaro were at the end of their last trail.

The country he'd been traversing, the Great Basin of the Utah Territory, was so wide open he could almost see tomorrow. It was mostly barren desert plains crosshatched by equally barren mountains. Jagged volcanic rock loomed black against the sky.

Fargo knew this area as the western limit of the U.S. Army's vast Department of the Platte. Ten years ago, as a contract scout, he had led a detail of military surveyors and mapmakers through the Wasatch Range. Mountain Utes laid siege to them, and only a few well-aimed "smudge pots" (fire bombs made for tossing) frightened them off.

Fargo, whom some called the Trailsman, had explored this region before and knew how to survive in it. Still, it didn't help when some cowardly would-be assassin had deliberately poisoned his water supply a week ago at a Humboldt River outpost west of here. And Fargo, though lacking proof, had a good idea, who had done it: Dill Stover, a barracks-room bully who pretended to be a soldier only to advance his criminal schemes.

Buckskins and beard powdered white from the alkali soil, Fargo led his played-out pinto stallion by the bridle reins. Fargo had lost his bearings in the last dust storm, but hoped like hell he was on the right path to reach the huge snowmelt reservoir at Mormon Station.

"That's the gait, old campaigner," Fargo remarked when the stallion lifted his nose into the furnace-hot wind. "We've got red sons all around us."

The Ovaro was trained to alert at the odor of bear grease, which many Indians smeared into their hair. Fargo knew he would require every possible warning because, unexpectedly, this entire region was crawling with warpath Indians.

This was terrain so hostile that even the mission padres gave it wide berth. Normally the Great Basin was empty except for a few nomadic braves, mostly

Utes and a few Paiutes or Shoshonis. Lately, though, somebody had been selling guns, amo, and liquor to the Utes. Now they were spreading terror through simultaneous raids on stage stations, mail riders, and freighters.

The Ovaro's ears pricked forward and Fargo drew his Colt, palming the wheel to check the loads. He'd rather face trouble on a tired horse than afoot, so Fargo stepped up into leather and loosened his brass-frame Henry in its boot.

"Keep up the strut," he urged the Ovaro, shortening the reins in case of trouble.

The pinto, like his master, was seriously dehydrated. Yet he brought his head up without fighting the bit, ready for the next scrape.

The wind rose to a shrieking howl, blasting Fargo's face with hard-driven grit and greatly reducing visibility. The brutal afternoon sun coaxed out a thick layer of sweat that mixed with the dust coating his skin, forming an irritating paste.

The Ovaro alerted again. Fargo, spotting dim shapes ahead in the swirling confusion, reached for his Henry, then checked the motion, his bearded jaw dropping open in astonishment.

"Dill goddamn Stover," he said aloud, the words surprised out of him.

The wind abated, and a strange sight revealed itself. Stover, in civilian clothes, sat his handsome roan gelding to one side of a buckboard heaped high with goods, including water casks. Stover bristled with arms: a shotgun, several revolvers, crossed bandoleers of bullets. A similarly armed guard covered the other side of the conveyance.

A driver wearing a broadcloth suit, and a hat with a veil to protect his eyes from grit and glare, was dickering with a skinny man who looked dead on his feet—bare, bleeding feet, at that.

"Fifteen dollars for a *glass* of water?" the man exclaimed. "Sir, that's usury!"

"No, pilgrim, it's the going price for water in the desert," the driver replied.

Fargo gaped at the four children. The youngest was on the verge of passing out, as was the exhausted-looking woman who was obviously expecting a child. And that compact little brunette beside her was staring at Fargo as if he were the Messiah arrived.

"Sir!" the man protested again. "We have no cash. We were robbed by a road gang east of here. At least give us water for the children."

"It's no skin off my ass what happens to those little shirttail brats. It's nothing personal, mister, just business discipline. If I give charity to one family, they all demand it. I'll take trade if you're cash-strapped."

"We lost our team, wagon, everything, south of here."

Fargo recalled a ruggedly built prairie wagon, and the dead team nearby, he'd spotted earlier. Just then Dill Stover, who'd been idly picking his teeth with a twig, shifted his trouble-seeking eyes in Fargo's direction. For a moment, before he reacted, he paled as if seeing a ghost. *Figured me for dead by now,* Fargo told himself.

He started to raise the scattergun, but instantly Fargo's right fist was curled around deadly steel. He thumb-cocked the hammer.

"Raise that smoke pole one more inch, Dill," Fargo promised him, "and you'll be kissing Satan's ass in hell. Goes for you, too, mister."

This last was directed at the second guard, a turkey-necked man with shifty eyes. He let his half-removed repeating rifle fall back into its saddle sheath.

"Is this a holdup?" demanded the driver. He seemed more amused than annoyed.

" 'Pears to me you're the one doing the robbing," Fargo replied, riding slowly back to glance in the buckboard. It was filled with footgear, clothing, and all sorts of food, even airtight tins of oysters and caviar.

"No law against a man setting his own prices based on demand," the driver replied. He pushed the veil aside and watched Fargo with the steady, unblinking eyes of a rattler.

"Especially," Fargo added, "with somebody poisoning all the water holes around here, huh? Creates a helluva demand."

His eyes shifted to Stover, who sat a silver-trimmed vaquero saddle he hadn't owned a week ago. "Just like somebody poisoned my water before I left the outpost at Mary's Station."

Stover's broad, blunt face twisted with insolence. "There was others there besides me. If I decide to kill a man, Fargo, I brace him toe to toe," his bullhorn voice rasped.

Fargo doubted that. Stover was shiftier than a creased buck. His tone right now was that of a man with an axe to grind, and clearly he meant to grind it until the wheel squeaked. Fargo had recently been forced to spend two months with the unlikable man, on a scouting expedition to sight through a federal resupply road for the U.S. Army's Far West outposts.

A rainy-day poker game at Mary's Station on the Humboldt had evolved into a dollar-ante slugfest between soldiers and scouts, and Fargo found himself riding a streak. Private Stover accused him of peeking at the deadwood. In the ensuing scuffle Fargo had severely pistol-whipped Stover instead of killing him— a serious mistake.

That beating, Fargo realized, was cankering at Stover. And the shotgun barrel was slowly coming up.

"You deserted, huh?" Fargo asked.

Stover looked smug. "Three-month enlistment, know-it-all."

Fargo believed that much. The army had to offer such foolish contracts now that goldfields dotted the West and drew off manpower.

"Well, next time you poison my gutbag of water with strychnine," Fargo advised him, "don't leave a little of the powder as a clue."

Stover had been making a cigarette. He struck a match and leaned into the flame, eyes mocking Fargo.

"Folks talk you up pretty high, Fargo," he said. "But you best watch that mouth of yours, hear? A man can turn his tongue into a shovel and dig his own grave with it."

"The ass waggeth his ears." Fargo glanced at the driver. "How 'bout it, boss man? Some water all around, starting with the tads?"

"No one asked you to put your oar in my boat, mister. If these pilgrims pay up, they're welcome to drink."

The driver glanced at the brunette, who still looked quite tempting despite the wear and tear of this desert hell. "I'm even willing to be flexible on the payment method," he added.

"Mighty Christian of you." Fargo watched turkey neck from the corner of one eye. The heavily armed man had a larval face with the furtive, hunted look of an owlhoot. And he was gradually turning his horse so that he and Stover could burn Fargo in a crossfire play. Never mind, thought Fargo, how many women and kids they would also mow down . . .

"You heading to Salt Lake for the big race, Fargo?"

Stover suddenly jeered. "The big race the Mormons're puttin' on? Me, I'd love to ride against you, cut you and that stallion down to size."

Who *hadn't* heard of the so-called Salt Lake Run, a grueling 120-mile horse race across brutal salt and volcanic-rock desert. No remounts allowed and no water except a tank at the halfway point and whatever the rider dared to carry. Besides a generous cash prize, the winner would be offered a lucrative contract to carry mail between Salt Lake City and the Mormon settlement of San Bernardino, California.

But Stover's question, Fargo realized, was only a diversion. A fox play was coming.

He looked at Stover, everything in Fargo's face smiling except those unblinking, lake-blue eyes. "Don't overrate yourself, Dill," he warned in a quiet, almost pleasant tone. The former soldier paled beneath his beard scruff.

Turkey neck chose that moment to make his play, expecting Stover to back his hand. Even as he slapped for a hog-leg pistol in an underarm holster, Fargo flipped his Colt into his left hand and raised his right leg, snatching the Arkansas Toothpick from his boot.

All this happened in an eyeblink. Turkey neck's big pistol cleared leather even as Fargo's right arm hurled the blade at him in a streaking blur. The Arkansas Toothpick punched deep into the man's chest before he could fire a shot. He twitched a few times, coughed up a gout of blood, then slid from the saddle like a sack of grain.

Fargo's Colt remained aimed at Stover, who sat stone still. But the Trailsman had forgotten about the driver of the buckboard—until he heard the loud, metallic click of a rifle being cocked.

No other series has this much historical action!

THE TRAILSMAN

#257:	COLORADO CUTTHROATS	0-451-20827-7
#258:	CASINO CARNAGE	0-451-20839-0
#259:	WYOMING WOLF PACK	0-451-20860-9
#260:	BLOOD WEDDING	0-451-20901-X
#261:	DESERT DEATH TRAP	0-451-20925-7
#262:	BADLAND BLOODBATH	0-451-20952-4
#263:	ARKANSAS ASSAULT	0-451-20966-4
#264:	SNAKE RIVER RUINS	0-451-20999-0
#265:	DAKOTA DEATH RATTLE	0-451-21000-X
#266:	SIX-GUN SCHOLAR	0-451-21001-8
#267:	CALIFORNIA CASUALTIES	0-451-21069-4
#268:	NEW MEXICO NYMPH	0-451-21137-5
#269:	DEVIL'S DEN	0-451-21154-5
#270:	COLORADO CORPSE	0-451-21177-4
#271:	ST. LOUIS SINNERS	0-451-21190-1
#272:	NEVADA NEMESIS	0-451-21256-8
#273:	MONTANA MASSACRE	0-451-21256-8
#274:	NEBRASKA NIGHTMARE	0-451-21273-8
#275:	OZARKS ONSLAUGHT	0-451-21290-8
#276:	SKELETON CANYON	0-451-21338-6
#277:	HELL'S BELLES	0-451-21356-4
#278:	MOUNTAIN MANHUNT	0-451-21373-4
#279:	DEATH VALLEY VENGEANCE	0-451-21385-8
#280:	TEXAS TART	0-451-21433-1
#281:	NEW MEXICO NIGHTMARE	0-451-21453-6
#282:	KANSAS WEAPON WOLVES	0-451-21475-7
#283:	COLORADO CLAIM JUMPERS	0-451-21501-X

Available wherever books are sold or at
www.penguin.com

The Pre-Civil War Series by
Jason Manning

War Lovers
0-451-21173-1
Retired war hero Colonel Timothy Barlow returns as
right-hand man to President Jackson when there's
trouble brewing on the border—trouble called the
Mexican-American War.

Apache Storm
0-451-21374-2
With Southern secession from the Union in the East,
the doomed Apaches in the West are determined to die
fighting. But Lt. Joshua Barlow is willing to defy the
entire U.S. Army to fight the Apaches on his own terms.

s666